26 Absurdities
of
Tragic Proportions

Matthew C. Woodruff

Cover design by Matt Woodruff
Stories edited by Gayle Michalak

ISBN13: 978-1720861751

Author's Note:

The inspiration for *26 Absurdities* came from the illustrative works of Edward Gorey.

Illustrator Edward Gorey has been described as "an extraordinary imagination," as being "a great American illustrator," and that "his works are equally amusing, somber, and nostalgic." No doubt his works partly inspired people like Tim Burton.

Everyone who sees Mr. Gorey's work has a strong opinion about it. The illustrations in his *Gashlycrumb Tinies* caught my attention at a young age and filled me with wonder at the type of imagination that could create such a dreadful masterpiece. For years I, no doubt like many of you, would wonder at the events that led up to the situations that caused these poor children's unusual deaths. How does one die of ennui, for example, or get sucked dry by leeches?

The following 26 short tales will explore, with some humor, the last few hours, days or weeks of the lives of these ill-fated children. As you read what fate or destiny had in store for them, you may believe it or you may discard it as you see fit.

One thing is certain though, once these tales are read, you will not forget these children.

Enjoy!

CONTENTS

I.	AMY	1.
II.	BASIL	9.
III.	CLARA	12.
IV.	DESMOND	17.
V.	ERNEST	22.
VI.	FANNY	27.
VII.	GEORGE	32.
VIII.	HECTOR	36.
IX.	IDA	41.
X.	JAMES	46.
XI.	KATE	51.
XII.	LEO	56.
XIII.	MAUD	60.
XIV.	NEVILLE	66.
XV.	OLIVE	70.
XVI.	PRUE	76.
XVII.	QUENTIN	81.
XVIII.	RHODA	86.
XIX.	SUSAN	91.
XX.	TITUS	96.
XXI.	UNA	100.
XXII.	VICTOR	105.
XXIII.	WINNIE	109.
XXIV.	XERXES	113.
XXV.	YORICK	115.
XXVI.	ZILLAH	121.

AMY

The house was one of those once grand and slowly falling apart places usually referred to as 'genteel'. The three story, white clapboard exterior was showing its age like an old drag queen – sagging soffits, bulging casements, peeling paint and trees and bushes badly in need of pruning, all combining for an air of futility and lethargy unseen since the latest round of Middle East peace talks. The house was a small microcosm of the whole neighborhood, in fact the whole town, which had seen better, younger and more vibrant days.

The more important businesses in Siena, Florida had long since moved down State Highway 27 with the fast food chains and drug stores. It being a marginally more prosperous area and importantly, an area frequented with more traffic. This exodus left behind a main street with a row of single story store fronts, largely infested by pawn shops, off market dollar stores, abandoned county health and legal offices, one old but miraculously still open IGA market with the 'G' missing since the hurricane of '67 (ask any old timer about it), cracking sidewalks and empty, sad spaces.

For Maria, it was perfect.

Maria was herself a small-town girl, brought-up in the northeast in a town that boasted one k-12 school, and two competing diners with $4.99 all-you-can-eat specials on alternating Thursdays. Maria was happy to now be able to raise her daughter in a similar, though slightly more depressing, small town environment.

It was Maria's *Grand Plan*, and Maria liked to have plans.

In elementary school, after watching a particularly weird b-rated sci-fi space saga, she wanted to be a robot. As a ninth grader, after seeing a revolutionary war reenactment, she wanted to be a general and in her senior year, for no apparent reason, Maria was going to be a boxer. As Maria's grandmother, who loved Maria's winsomeness with all her heart, once said to her, "It's nice to have plans dear, but yours are just so… inappropriate."

Maria didn't think in terms of appropriate or inappropriate or expected or logical. Maria thought with her heart. Her full-bodied beating heart. And for Maria, at least currently more than anything else, she wanted to open a Bed & Breakfast.

Maria had read an article in a magazine at the lawyer's office which was handling her grandmother's estate (if that's what you could call it) that said B&B's were on the rise. Instantly Maria knew in her heart of hearts, this is what she wanted 'more than anything,' her own B&B in a small town for her and her daughter, Amy.

This fit in perfectly with a TV show Maria had seen last week on a travel channel that said tourism in Florida was as strong as ever, even with the bad economy. In Maria's mind here was the answer to her heart-of-hearts plan, which she had for a whole 15 minutes, open a B&B in a small town in Florida. No thought given to whether or not Amy wanted to be pulled out of her current school half a nation away, and away from her friends to move to a ramshackle and rambling old house, probably haunted (Maria hoped – more interesting for her imagined guests) and be conscripted into the hospitality industry.

At first Maria searched the internet for an existing B&B in Florida that be for sale, but soon realized the money from her grandmother's meager estate would not be nearly enough. After mentioning her depressing and futile search to her friend Allison, her off-hand comment, 'wouldn't it be great to start one up from scratch?' sent Maria off on a whole new search with a whole new mission and a slightly modified *Grand Plan*. She would look for a large, old house, preferably furnished that had potential. The latter criteria was the least important because in Maria's mind her plan was a sure success. She and Amy could make all the potential it would need.

Now, as I'm sure you can imagine, trying to research and buy something on the internet, like a grand old home, is difficult to say the least. Dozens of emails and follow-up phone calls to incredulous, over-worked, under-compensated realtors (or under-worked, over-compensated, as the case may be) and testy, despondent or just plain bored, 'For Sale by Owners' might leave any one of us just plain worn out.

But Maria was not.

I would like to say that 'perseverance' was Maria's middle name (it's actually Prudence, after her grandmother of course) but Maria's history at not becoming a robot or a general or a boxer is fairly indicative of how long Maria's usual plans endure, that is to say, until the first roadblock or sometimes until the next *Grand Plan* presents itself.

Maria got lucky though fairly early in her search, (or not lucky, as you'll see when events unfold). Maria stumbled onto some very motivated sellers. This group of five siblings were strangely in agreement with each other as to how quickly to dispose of their elderly mother's (now passed) old house and old furnishings located in a town none of them cared to live in, or even very much to reminisce about.

Enter the Bidlers. The five Bidler sisters, all still named Bidler due to tear-heaving, gut-wrenching divorces or just plain homeliness and/or orneriness, ranged in age from the early 40's to the mid-60's. (The old woman herself was 84 when she passed.) Motivated doesn't begin to describe their attitude toward selling their mother's run-down, infested and smelly ramshackle, drafty old house (and those were its good qualities)!

Not that they could be blamed for their attitudes. After all the old lady died in this house and stunk it up for four days before any neighbor thought to check on her and search for a daughters' phone number. The old lady's essence continued to linger in it. Plus, it may have been four or forty years since the last good cleaning, who could tell? The Bidler sisters visited a little as possible. It was actually hard to even tell what color anything was anymore.

The initial call went something like this:

Hopeful Maria: "I'm calling about the house you have listed on Craigslist, and I have a few..."

A Bidler (as they have gotten older they are harder to tell apart, all being kind of nasally, frumpy and round) abruptly said: "We can't finance."

Maria, only slightly taken aback by the tone: "Um, I have some money. Actually, my grandmot..."

A Bidler (or the other, there may have been multiple ones on the call) in the sweetest tone now that the magic *money* words were spoken: "We'd love to show you the house, it was such a great old place."

Maria, now getting flustered: "Um, I'm not actually in Florida, yet."

The you know whos: "Then how are you gonna see the place?"

"I thought if you could maybe email me some more photos and describe it to me, I could mail you a check? Um, you know, a cashier's check I mean. I want to open a B&B," Maria finished in a rush. This was the first time she divulged her *Grand Plan* to anyone outside her little circle.

Now, something that has rarely happened in the history of man (ask any of their ex-husbands) a Bidler sister was left momentarily speechless. Never in their wild imaginings did any of them think some poor sap… er, I mean buyer, would want to buy it sight unseen. *Probably the only way they could sell it*, one or all of them thought to themselves upon hearing the news, and certainly not for… a what, a B&B did she say? "Broken-down and bereft," one of them later guffawed after seeing the check with her own eyes. Sadly, the others all pretty much agreed, but it wasn't their problem anymore.

"That would be perfectly acceptable," she twittered. A Bidler sister twittering is not a nice sound, kind of like a strangled frog. "It's furnished you know, turn of the century, quite modern for its time." Which century or which time was better left undiscovered.

Though it was a little more complicated, with a lawyer and a survey being needed, a title search and all the other things that encumber real estate transactions, that's how Maria and Amy ended up moving to Siena, Florida to own their own B&B.

Part 2

I don't need to remind you, poor Amy had no say in any of this. As she had never had in any of Maria's *Grand Plans*. Not the time Maria invested a good portion of their meager resources in bulk glass and stone beads when Amy was five (home jewelry making business). Amy almost choked to death on the brightly colored little things. (They found two boxes of them stuffed back in a closet when packing for Florida.) Nor the time when Amy was eight and Maria thought it would be a good idea to move in with her current boyfriend. He was a nice enough fellow though probably not too bright himself. Unfortunately he lived in a studio apartment, so it didn't quite work out as hoped. Nor the time, …well you get the idea. Amy was blown on the winds of Maria's Grand Plans, like a sparrow in a hurricane or in this case, like the 'G' in the old IGA sign.

Amy tried to make the best of it, after her tearful goodbyes and heartfelt "I'll write every day!" to her best friends. After all, what choice did she have? Amy was nothing if not practical where her mother was concerned. It was gonna happen, period.

Amy used to wistfully imagine having a family like many of her friends had, a father who worked and came home and helped her with homework and took her fishing on the weekends, a mother who baked cookies and taught her how to apply makeup. Maria did once have the idea to bake lots of cookies and sell them at a farmer's market, but the facts that Maria didn't really know how to bake from scratch and knew nothing about the health department or licensing, caused that particular plan to not quite work out. They ate a lot of funny looking cookies though, so that was fun. Anyway, when it was time to go to Florida, Amy was ready.

You remember the opening of the old TV show "Alice", where she and her son pack up their car and move to start a new life? Well it was kind of like that, except Alice had a much nicer car.

Part 3

'Welcome to Siena, Florida' the sign used to say, Amy supposed. It was kinda hard to tell. Amy and her mother made the trip in only three days, with little or no difficulties and passed over the 'city' line and past the sign, late in the afternoon, just as the sun was touching the western horizon. Interestingly, in Florida unlike New York for example, all municipal areas are either counties or cities, no townships, no villages and no boroughs. The designation is not dependent on size. A city in Florida can be any size. Siena was, as previously discussed, smaller than most and more sorrowful looking then the rest of small town America.

Amy was however trying to look forward to this new adventure, after all, this is the first time they would own their own place, so that was something special Amy supposed. And they weren't *forever* from the beach. This being Florida, a beach was never more than two hours away. Amy doesn't know much about the beach, but her friends thought it was a good thing, so she was looking forward to it.

As they drove through town and down the main street, a normal person, or shall we say, a person without Maria's enthusiasm for her *Grand Plan*, would have noticed the rundown and dilapidated feel of the town. Not Maria, what Maria saw and thought was, *here is where the new café will open after they see all my guests*, while

5

gazing at an empty corner location and *there's a perfect spot for the row of little boutiques my guests will shop in*, looking at the mostly empty block, and etc. Enthusiasm and imagination were convincing Maria of her success.

The house was not hard to find being only two blocks off the main street. They pulled up in front and stared out the car windows at a long, broken sidewalk in a badly overgrown, weed infested yard. It lead up to a set of five deteriorating cement steps that may have at one time had iron handrails, ending on a large grey roundish porch. Its narrow round, once painted columns were centered by a large, ugly dark brown set of doors, framed by two long dusty looking windows, too dirty to see through.

Maria loved it, it was exactly as she pictured. She could already see it full of happy guests. Amy, well she was trying, but to say she was a little disappointed is not saying enough. One small sigh though is all she let escape as she forlornly gazed at her future.

They opened the car doors and Amy started to get stuff out. "Leave that stuff, come on, let's go right in" Maria shouted as she vaulted from the car and up the sidewalk. Amy, who was wrestling to extricate a suitcase from the dangerously over-packed back seat abandoned it and ran to catch up, narrowly avoiding tripping and cracking her head open on the outdoor steps.

"Amy," Maria admonished for the hundredth time, "watch where you are going. Some day you are gonna fall to your death if you're not more careful!" Amy rolled her eyes, but so her mother couldn't see.

They stopped in front of the peeling, strangely lopsided double doors. To the right of the door on the porch and under a rock was a large manila envelope as promised by the Bidlers, containing some papers to be signed by Maria and a set of five keys. All the keys were the same, one happily contributed by each Bidler sister and all for the front door. If there were any other keys for any other doors, they had been lost in the dustiness of time.

Now I would like to say that the inserting of the key and opening of the front door for the first time was a magical and profound experience for Maria and Amy, so I will. It was a magical and profound experience. Here was proof that one of Maria's *Grand Plans* for her and Amy was about to come true. Maria had purchased her first house, her happiness at this moment was deep and fulfilling, her gratitude to her grandmother for making it possible was absolute, and rightly so on both counts.

How was Amy feeling? Well she was a practical young lady.

After a little struggle with the lock and sticky door (it's the humidity), Maria pushed the doors wide open, bathing the entry hall in the dying afternoon light. Immediately they both were awestruck at the vision of the two-story grand staircase that filled the center of the three-story entryway, as anyone other than the Bidlers would be. This was old time southern elegance at its best, run down perhaps but majestic nonetheless.

Why, you ask, had there been no photos of this majestic staircase included in Maria's emails from the Bidlers? Simply put, the Bidlers were all over-weight and tired, and they loathed the idea of waddling up and down those stairs. They felt two stories of stairs was not a selling point. Old lady Bidler herself hadn't been up those stairs in years.

Even the ancient and decaying smell that charged out and assaulted Maria and Amy couldn't diminish the majesty of the central stair. For a brief second Amy felt optimistic about the future in this old house. Amy instantly loved the staircase, with its rich mahogany bannisters and dark deep pile carpeting, that wound up and up with a grand window on every landing. Amy got dizzy following it all the way up with her eyes.

This staircase has seen many things, none of which it can talk about. It saw new babies carried gingerly up its heights. It saw at least two young ladies, dressed in all the finery imaginable come down on the way to greet their nervous, bespeckled and acne ridden prom dates. The staircase even saw one young lady come down to get married on the bottom step, with a long flowing train all in white. It also saw the same girls running back up in tears, after dates, engagements or marriages gone wrong. It sat silent as the hopes and dreams of these five young ladies were dashed on the cruel realities of their lives.

It has been a long time since it has seen hope and joy, like on Maria's face and now on Amy's.

"Oh Mom, it's great," Amy gushed, hugging Maria's neck just before she launched herself up the stairs, marveling at the softness of the carpet and the feel of the smooth age-worn wood of the bannister.

Amy didn't notice the flaws, the cobwebs and dust, the cracking and peeling paint or the worn spots on the carpet. Amy only saw a new hope. She stopped and looked out every window, drinking in her and Maria's new life. Just as the sun set for good beyond the western horizon, Amy stopped at the top of the great staircase and turned around maybe just a little bit too fast, to go back down, to hug her mother again, and to start their new adventure.

Sadly, for Amy and Maria, this *was* the first time the staircase saw death as Amy tripped and tumbled down to the bottom floor. Destiny or fate once again smashing all of Maria's hopes for her *Grand Plan*.

The End.

BASIL

Basil's Mother is a scientist, not just any kind of scientist, but a quantum physicist. Basil doesn't know what that means, but why should he when he's only eight years old?

Basil and his mother live in Russia. They are in fact Russian. Not everyone who lives in Russia is Russian, some are Georgian, some are Chechyan, some are French, like anywhere some people had come from other places.

But not Basil's family, they have always lived in Russia. Before Basil was born it was known as the Union of Soviet Socialist Republics (USSR) and it had many different territories. All the people in the area were referred to as Russians or Soviets. Now it is known as Russia. And (in some minds) it is not as big or as great but all the people who are born there are Russians, and still proud.

Back when it was the USSR, everyone worked for the government, more or less, especially the scientists and everything was paid for, more or less. Now Basil's mother works at a University. Many of the older Russians long for the day the USSR is whole again, and is great once again, but not Basil's mother. Though she is old (she had Basil when she was 61) and remembers the days of the communist USSR, she thinks the new Russia is better than the old. She doesn't have to work on what she is told to work on and now she can work on whatever she can get funding for.

In her spare time Basil's mother built a time machine. She couldn't get funding for her time machine the normal way. Truth is she didn't even try. Who would give some crazy, old Russian scientist money to build a time machine? That's why Basil's mother had to build it at home, in the garage. They do have garages in Russia, just like anywhere else. Apparently, they also have time machines, just like nowhere else.

Another famous scientist named Albert Einstein, who was in fact not Russian, said time travel was not possible. Albert believed everything happened at once, so how could you travel to a time that is currently happening? Basil's Mother didn't believe Albert was correct, though.

Basil's mother had an idea of how time travel would be possible. She believed, unlike Albert, that time was a straight road, maybe a little bumpy at times but you could see behind you and in front of you and just like on a road, you can stop and go backwards or go faster and go frontwards.

To build her time machine, she just needed the parts. Even in Russia, you don't just go to the corner store and buy a flux capacitor or whatever the thingy is that makes time travel possible. Basil's mother had to build what she needed and that costs money, lots of it. Some people call it funding. When you are trying to steal it though it is not usually referred to as funding. But how does an aging Russian quantum physicist acquire (i.e. steal) a large sum of money in a short time?

By defrauding the government, of course.

Now by its very nature, the government has access to a lot of money. And as one of the world's leading quantum physicists, Basil's mother knew only a few of her peers could ever understand her work. She figured if she made her grant applications seem reasonable enough, while promising wonderful things, she could get all the money she needed.

Stealth technology for battleships? Consider it done, Cha-Ching! Quantum powered spy satellites that move at high speed and last virtually forever? Consider it done, Cha-Ching! Better erectile dysfunction management? Consider it done, Cha-Ching! And etc. Cha-Ching!

Basil's mother was smart. She had a foolproof plan. She would defraud the money she needed in the *now*, then after her time machine was operational she would go to the past or the future and recoup all the money she would need to build her time machine and travel back to *before now*, give herself the money and use that money to build her time machine without having to defraud the government. She was only wondering why she hadn't visited herself yet with the money. But maybe she has to do the whole thing the first time to start the loop off. Nobody understood time travel as well as Basil's mother so that is to say, nobody understood time travel. Just because you or I can bake a soufflé (well, you may be able to, I certainly can't) doesn't mean we understand why the whole is better than the parts. It just is.

Basil's mother built a time machine in her garage by defrauding massive amounts of money from the government. Surprisingly or not, everything didn't go exactly as planned.

Even though Basil was only eight years old, being the son of one of the world's leading quantum physicists, he was pretty smart. It shouldn't be a big surprise to learn Basil knew how to operate his mother's time machine. He was after all, always watching her tinker. It was interesting. What poor Basil didn't know was how to fend off hungry bears. So, when Basil got into his mother's time machine and accidentally travelled 250 years into the past and stepped out of his mother's time machine into the cold Russian woods, well let's just say the bears were happy and now not so hungry.

Basil's mother now lives in an asylum, after being arrested for defrauding massive amounts of money from the government. Her insistence that she used the money to build a time machine and that her eight year old son must have taken it *somewhen*, and was also missing seemed a bit too, let's say, *eccentric* to the prosecutor, who believed only a crazy woman would defraud massive amounts of money from the government and kill, or sell (who really knew) her own son and claim to have built a time machine to cover it all up.

Though she really seemed to believe it.

Russia has asylums because Russia has crazy people who commit crimes and believe fantastical stories to account for the mundane, just like everywhere else.

Russian stories always have a moral. Cinderella, another Russian story for example, had a moral. A moral of a story is the reason why you should or shouldn't always do the thing the story talks about.

Basil's story has a moral. It should be obvious. Don't travel back in time to the Russian woods in a time machine if you can't fend off bears, or Cossacks too, probably. It might be good to note that travelling forward in time also may have hazards, even if you don't run into bears or Cossacks.

The End.

CLARA

Part 1

It was April 27th, in the year of our Lord 1828. A big event in the City of London, the greatest city in the world, was about to unfold. It was the opening of the London Zoo, the only one of its kind in the world. The London Zoo was primarily for scientific research but Clara's Father, Henry, was the chief keeper, an important and respected working-class position.

Henry wasn't always chief keeper. It was a new position and title created for the zoo and for Henry, who through a judicious and perhaps a ridiculous amount of hard work, respectful subservience to his 'betters', a shrill and nagging wife, and a strange knack of caring for wild animals, merited a promotion. When Clara was born in 1818 as the first of Henry's four living children, Henry was a mere clark in the Tower of London, where his father had secured a position for him when he announced he was to marry. He stayed a clark for many years, doing things of a clarkly nature and helping out with the animal menagerie, which was then housed at the Tower.

That whole rainy and cold month of April 1828, temporary workers, mostly from the docks, dressed in their wool pants and shabby collarless once white shirts under their dirty vests, (more often than not with missing buttons) and with their workmen's caps skewed on their heads, were busy up and down London streets transporting animals in large and small wooden crates and iron cages, on horse drawn carts or hand pulled or pushed wagons from the Tower of London menagerie, or from one or two donated private collections. Under Henry's direction and through workers strikes, sickness, mobs and bureaucratic entanglements, a job that would eventually take four years to finally complete.

A Londoner of the time could easily see their routes by merely following the hay and animal droppings spread through-out the cities cobblestoned streets and alleys. Past Billingsgate, past St. Paul's Cathedral, through neighborhoods like Holborn, Covent Garden, Fitrozia and onto Regent's Park where the new zoo was to be located on donated land.

12

Henry was ecstatic. Even his wife momentarily stopped complaining about Henry's lack of upward mobility and income. Maybe now they could abandon their rented second floor flat in Paddington that started to smell suspiciously and embarrassingly like curry and finally move up in the world, maybe to Gloucester Street with others of a certain taste and income where Henry's wife imagined they belonged. No matter it would be farther from Regent's Park and closer to the Tower than where they resided now. (If only their accents and manners followed suit, but that is a different problem for a different day.)

So, move they did to Gloucester Street, or near enough that Henry's wife could say she lived on Gloucester street anyway. There the ladies weren't as welcoming to Henry's wife and family as they might have wished. In fact, several of them looked down their noses at them, as it were. A phrase that may have originated with these particular ladies, judging from the size of their noses. But Henry's wife's old friends from the *old* neighbourhood of Paddington were suitably impressed and more importantly, jealous.

Clara didn't care one way or the other what neighbourhood they resided in. In fact, Clara disapproved of the whole class structure, a forward thinking and independent young lady if ever there was one.

After the debacle of getting all the animals moved and housed, the scientific labs set-up, the researchers invited or appointed, the constant hay and food deliveries scheduled and maintained and a million other things Henry was suddenly responsible for, it was now 1832.

Part 2

Clara was now fourteen. As a young pre-Victorian woman, Clara's family hadn't been in a position to get her any formal education, though her younger two brothers, Henry and Edward, twelve and eight respectively, went half a day three days a week to the priests for some writing and arithmetic and history now that Henry could afford it. Fourteen was a good marrying age. Henry's wife had done her best to prepare Clara in household management though Clara remained unnaturally stubborn concerning some things, and Henry had his eye out for a respectable man of employment or of certain means for Clara. Certainly, Clara's chances were for a much better match now that they lived near Gloucester Street than if they had stayed in Paddington. There was only one small issue. Clara didn't want to get married.

Clara wanted to make a difference in the world. Clara insisted she wanted to help out those poor men at a workhouse near their old neighborhood, maybe by working in the soup kitchen. While Henry may have unwillingly obliged her, her mother said no in no uncertain terms, with foot down, hands on hips and a disturbing scowl on her face that after all these years Henry knew the ramifications of. Could you imagine? Our daughter around men of that type? What would the neighbors think? The conversation was short, the tears and recriminations were not.

If Clara could have read or gone to school she might have heard of the Fabians, a group of like-minded free thinkers who wanted and advocated for social improvement. She might have had a specific cause, and not just been blown on the winds of her own radical (for the time) thinking and un-clarified desires for betterment, feeling lost and unfulfilled. Unfortunately, their own societal upbringing, trappings and lack of formal education prevented her parents from understanding what was happening inside of Clara.

Henry's wife was now in a hurry to get Clara married and settled. Suddenly, Sunday after church dinners sported young men of a certain type, slyly introduced to Clara as 'a nephew of old Mrs. What's-her-name, from the butcher's shop'. Or simply, 'John Somebody who works with your father's friend'. Or 'Mr. Respectable, his uncle is a barrister'. The parade of men, young and not so young was full of handsome stumbling morons and homely, engaging conversationalists and everything in between. Any one of them would have felt lucky to catch Clara's interest, an attractive woman of strong conviction from a respectable family. But Clara was having none of it.

After a while, when the list of possible suitors was growing thin, Sunday evenings, after the selected guest of the week departed, was full of more tears and recriminations. Henry's wife was becoming desperate. That is when Henry stumbled on to a great idea. Clara could come to work with him at the zoo a few days a week. Clara loved animals, a trait inherited from Henry himself, no doubt. After all, there were several suitable men working at the zoo. Some were researchers, some were clarks, and some of them were single. Clara may fall in love with one based on a mutual interest and even though Clara's mother didn't put much stock in falling in love, who knows?

Though initially opposed to the idea, after all in pre-Victorian London respectable women didn't work out of the home, except for the occasional spinster teacher or nurse, Henry's wife haltingly agreed, not seeing any other way forward.

Henry was right on one account, Clara was thrilled with the idea, not for the chance to meet a possible suitor, no, but the chance to be around the animals her father (in her young mind) lovingly cared for.

From day one though, Clara was taken aback with revulsion. This was after all, a scientific study zoo. The animals were, well, studied. Their living conditions were barbaric. Here were monkeys from deepest, darkest Africa, intelligent and funny animals crammed together in cages too small, living in their own filth, dirty and smelly. There were big cats too, but these were mean and scared creatures, they were considered noble, loyal creatures in Clara's mind and weren't for study or cruel treatment. There were bears, which Clara had never seen before, but imagined as majestic wilderness rulers. These were snarling and mean, with matted fur and emaciated bodies. There was a grand lion, donated by some down on his luck explorer, who now lay listlessly throughout the day and night.

The list goes on, much in the same way of unloved, mistreated animals, fed and watered yes, but generally uncared for and occasionally put to some gruesome test.

Clara's revulsion turned to anger. How dare her father, the man she imagined cared for these majestic animals, treat them so? She insisted, no, demanded her father improve their lot with bigger cages, better care, no more cruel study, even, dare she utter the word... freedom.

Henry's heart was broken, he could see the revulsion in his daughter's eyes. Eventually Clara stopped going to the zoo. She couldn't even look at her father the same way again. She became depressed and despondent over her inability to improve the lives of these poor animals. If she couldn't even help a few poor dumb animals, how could she ever hope to help any needy people? She took her father's unwillingness to help them as a personal repudiation, not understanding there was nothing poor Henry could do as he was merely a minor functionary in a massive bureaucracy.

Clara stopped going to the zoo, stopped going outside completely. She stopped caring for her appearance and she stopped eating. Cajoling, demanding and pleading had no effect. Leeches and blistering gave no relief and resulted in nothing except to drain meager savings.

Finally one day, either due to weakness or a total and abject despondency, Clara could no longer leave the bed. Eventually they moved her to the divan in the parlor for a change of scenery, but it didn't matter, Clara was finished.

The family was never the same after that. Henry's job performance suffered greatly, as he now saw his animals through Clara's eyes and himself as ineffectual. He started spending every evening in the local pub. One drunken night he even tried to return to the zoo to release all the animals, thankfully only falling over drunk in a ditch instead. It wasn't long before a particularly industrious assistant took over Henry's post and Henry was let go. It was a devastating blow in the 1830's, with no social network to rely upon.

Henry Jr. and Edward had to leave their schooling and take menial jobs to help support the family. The family moved back to Paddington, where Henry's wife took in laundry and sewing to help make ends meet. The youngest contracted cholera and died. Their once upon time friends gazed upon them only with pity in their eyes now, no longer jealousy.

Their lives had now become irreparably broken, with Clara's demise.

The End.

DESMOND

Winter came early that year, before Thanksgiving even. A beautiful sight, looking west out the parlor's grand windows into Central Park. The snow glistening on the tree branches, piled on the tops of the stone walls, swirling in the light of the new electric street lamps.

The electric lights had been installed just that year, over the objection of the superstitious who thought electricity was a vapor that would eventually kill them if breathed in for too long. A thought that made Eloise Winters laugh. She understood electricity. She had gone to the World's Columbian Exposition and seen the great man, Nikolai Tesla's inventions. She knew it would change the world, which is why she convinced her husband, a well to do banker, to invest heavily with Tesla. She had even had the opportunity to speak to Tesla, a chance encounter yes, when her scarf had fallen to the floor of one of the exhibits. Tesla himself had chanced to be the one to secure and return it to her as he was passing by. The conversation short, a "Thank you" from her and a returned tip of the head and "Madame", from him. But she looked in his eyes and understood his mind, she'd like to say at dinner parties afterwards.

Eloise was pregnant again in her fifth or sixth month, they thought. *Thank God*, she thought suddenly as she put her hand to her expanding belly. No respectable New York family has just one child. She had already miscarried two others, but this one felt different. She was sure this time it would all work out, as had her first, Desmond, named after her husband's grandfather. An easy birth, but contrary to all known conventions of the time, Desmond was a wild, seemingly fearless boy. Easy birth, easy child, everyone knew but not Desmond. His tutors often quit in disgust, his nanny helplessly out maneuvered on most occasions, the household staff wary of his presence, the carriage horses even shied away from him. Though gentle Desmond would never harm a whisker on their heads.

Eloise's husband wanted to get one of the new horseless carriages that are powered by steam, of all things. Eloise was skeptical. How would steam pull a carriage? The few she had seen seemed to be stopped more often than in motion. She gave them a wide berth at any rate, clicking her teeth all the while. Still looking out the window, she noticed the street was emptier than most nights. The weather she supposed.

A chill moved through Eloise, starting low and slowly rolling up and through her. She pulled her shawl closer around and glanced over at the fireplaces just to see them burning gaily. A draft then, she supposed. She reached to ring for the servants in order to have them check that all the windows and doors were secure. Then she remembered they were all off to some new show despite the unexpected weather, this being their half night off. What a bother it was. A spot of tea would be perfect right now, or hot chocolate. Desmond loved hot chocolate. She could hear him playing with his toy soldiers in the dining room, where he knew he wasn't supposed to play. She suddenly didn't know what came over her, letting all the servants go off at once, when usually one or two always stayed. She was just too soft, she clicked to herself.

Eloise supposed she could manage a tray of hot chocolate on her own, and maybe a biscuit or two for her and Desmond. Eloise's husband was usually out late, stopping at his club for dinner and a game most evenings unless guests were expected, so he wasn't at home either. Suddenly her stomach growled at the thought of some of Mrs. Baskin's wonderful raisin biscuits. "Oh Dear" she laughed with a hand over her mouth. She headed to the back stairs to go down to the kitchens, clutching her shawl closed with one hand.

As she stepped onto the first downstairs landing she suddenly felt a little light-headed and stopped with her free hand on the railing for support. *Oh My!*, she thought, *I hope I'm not coming down with a cold.* She relieved her anxiety by determining that tomorrow she would spend the day in bed, with a steam pot – *now there was a good use for steam*, she clicked to herself.

She continued her downstairs journey, only to be suddenly brought up short by a brief, sharp pain lancing through her belly, like a fire running through her. She felt unaccountably hot and thirsty now. Fear immediately welled up in her. Fear for her unborn child, not herself. She was halfway down, should she continue down or go back up, she was caught in indecision. "Oh, where are those damn servants?" She uttered under her breath. The usage of the curse word, the strongest she knew, a sure sign of her growing desperation and fear.

The pain was brief, but scary. She should send for the doctor, but who would go? There is no one. He was all the way across the park and it was getting darker by the moment and snowing besides. Eloise didn't know what to do, rarely had she ever had to make her own important decisions. Decisions about what cloth to order for a new dress, yes. What staff to hire, yes, how to manage a charity, easy things, but not this.

She realized for the first time that she could no longer hear Desmond's little dining room war.

She could make it to the front door, she supposed and ask a passerby for help. Maybe there would even be a constable nearby. One of them could fetch the doctor. The plan stabilized and motivated her, bringing relief from uncertainty. As she turned to go back upstairs, she decided she could leave the door ajar and lay on the sofa in the parlor to wait for the doctor. It would be unseemly but she knew she just couldn't make it up to the third floor master suite, and there were no servants to give the doctor egress into the house.

As she clung to the railing for support and turned to make the trek up, a warm, wet feeling invaded her thighs and legs. "Oh No!" she cried out. "Not yet, I'm barely six months!" Her water had broken. She felt faint, but she had to see if there was blood mixed in. She steadied herself, leaning against the wall and put her shaking hand down her under garments and pulled it back out, wet, warm and pink. She couldn't help herself, she started to cry. Eloise now felt totally helpless, bereft and alone. It was going to happen again.

As soon as his mother had started out for the downstairs kitchen, Desmond set himself to stalking her. Going to the kitchen could only mean one thing, a treat was on its way. He snuck around corners and hid behind the dark, oversize furniture as his mother made her way through the Butler's Pantry to the back stairs. The maids hated to be stalked by Desmond, occasionally shrieking in fear when he pounced out laughing, the nanny glowering when she finally found him. His mother enjoyed their little games. Desmond was just high spirited in her opinion.

Desmond knew something was wrong, right at the outset. Desmond was a watcher as well as a doer. He noticed things, like the way his Mother clutched her shawl tight and looked a little wobbly but not as bad as a few of the nights his papa came home from his club when Desmond was hiding in the dressing room, but wobbly none the less.

When his mother grabbed for the railing, Desmond knew deep down something was wrong. He almost shouted out, "Mama!" but withheld himself. She needed something more, but what? Desmond's ten year old brain whirled furiously. What would papa do? He would shout for Baxter, their butler. But Baxter wasn't even home. What would Baxter do? *Think*, Desmond demanded to himself, and then like a revelation it came to him.

The doctor is what his mother needed, the smelly old Doctor Wallingsworth, whom Desmond hated lived and worked almost directly across the park Desmond knew as he had been there many times. But the park was big and dark at night. He was told to never, ever go into the park alone. Desmond, who really didn't feel fear (he had a condition that would later become known as Urbach-Wiethe disease) knew he needed a plan.

There is only one way to get across the park on a snowy dark night in a hurry, the carriage. But the carriage was too big for Desmond to handle alone. Frustration, which Desmond could feel, was starting to kick in. *Wait*, Desmond thought to himself, *the sleigh*! One horse can pull it easily and it fairly flies over the snow!

Now with a plan in hand, Desmond was energized. He bolted to the back of the house, pulled on his boots which were kept in a closet by the back door and ran out the door to the carriage house, slipping and sliding all the way. With his white breath puffing out from him, he ran to the carriage house where the horses, carriages and the sleigh were kept without any thought of personal danger.

Desmond suddenly realized he was very cold. Once in the carriage house the first thing Desmond did after lighting a lantern (the carriage house didn't yet have electric lights) was put on an old fur coat of his, a long scarf and a hat. His mother would kill him if he got a cold and would make him lay in bed all day with a smelly steam pot.

There was the sleigh, gleaming smartly in the middle of the floor in front of the carriage, thank goodness. It was just today taken out of storage and readied for winter. There was only one horse Desmond really trusted, Old Lady, and that old nag should have been put out to pasture long ago but Desmond insisted she stay, so here she still was. Desmond felt confident he knew how to get Old Lady hooked up to the sleigh. He didn't actually but had seen it done many times in the past. There were just one or two little things he might have overlooked. Nonetheless, it seemed to work.

Desmond unlatched and pushed the carriage house doors open, got into the sleigh and whooshed for Old Lady to go, and go she did. She already knew the route to the park herself, as that is the only place she's allowed to go anymore. Off she went into the park, towing an excited Desmond.

Desmond wasn't scared but he was in a hurry, so he pushed Old Lady to go faster and faster and the old thing did the best she could. After several near-misses on the slippery stone paths, they exited the other side of the treacherous ride through the park a little south of where Desmond thought the doctor's house was. He turned Old Lady north onto the street, stood fully erect and started calling out, "Doctor, Doctor". The few people out stopped and wondered at the young boy in the fast-moving sleigh shouting for a doctor.

It was a miracle that Doctor Wallingsworth was outside just at the time, coming home from his surgery. Just as he saw, heard and recognized Desmond and just as Desmond saw the doctor and started to shout out about his Mother, a deep feeling of relief passed through him. Then a terrible thing happened. A steam powered car careened into the track of Old Lady, no doubt having lost control on the slippery street. Old Lady bucked and reared up in abject fear, throwing Desmond up and out of the back of the sleigh, his scarf waving like a flag in the wind, onto his head.

Though this story seems sad, the night Desmond passed, his bravery and Old Lady's dash through the park did save his mother and baby sister. Once the doctor determined Desmond's final condition he immediately turned to the constable nearest him and exclaimed, "I have to get across the park right now my good man, lives are at risk! Take me in your police carriage!"

The constable obliged without further ado, with an "as you say, Sir" and another dash was made through the dark and treacherous park, but this time in the capable and experienced hands of the constable and police horses. When they arrived at Desmond's home, the doctor found the front door ajar and upon entering found Eloise half on and half off the sofa in the parlor in the throes of a difficult and nasty labor. For Eloise was wrong about what was happening and about how pregnant she really was. After a long and trying birth, Eloise had a daughter, who with her mother most surely would have expired had not poor, fearless Desmond fetched the doctor in time.

The End.

Ernest

There was never any official explanation as to how our poor little Ernest choked to death on his peach, but everyone had their suspicions I reckon.

Never to see him romp about the lawns again playing soldier or beg to be taken out in the boat. Never to see his face beam with delight when he spied his favorite dessert coming up from the kitchens, or the guilty look on his face when we would catch him in the cupboards late at night. It just tears my heart out, it does, to think of our poor little Ernest alone now, in the cold and unforgiving ground. Snuffed out at such a young, hopeful age. But poor little Ernest never had much hope in life, now did he? He was better off with God.

I guess I should start at the beginning, I should. Poor little Ernest come to us, oh nary on six months gone from then, I'd say. Come to us from the orphanage, where he was left after his mama passed on, God rest her soul. Alone and frightened, he was standing in that big doorway wearing his ratty old coat, leaky shoes and hat, clutching his one little bag for all he was worth. Voice quiet and shaky. That's how I first saw him.

Not once in those six months, as the Lord is my witness, did any in the family cast a kind gaze on our poor little Ernest or speak a warm consoling thought to 'im. Why the master even made the poor little tyke take his meals alone he did. And in that big dining room at that big table sitting so tiny in that big chair and not till after the rest of 'em dined. He wouldn't even let the poor little Ernest eat down with us when I asked.

"What?" the master gruffed through billowing clouds of blue pipe smoke, "He isn't a servant, he's in my fostercare. Can't be done, wouldn't be proper, hmpf".

As if starving the poor boy for a glimmer of affection is proper. I may just be a cook, but I'm a Christian not liked thems upstairs. Not if Christian charity and feeling is any show of it. Forgive me Lord, but it's the God's honest truth, it is.

I cried for days after our poor little Ernest passed on, though I tried to 'ide it from old Mr. 'im. "Egads, woman," the old Mr'd say, "Give it a rest" 'e said to me with his white whiskers twitching looking jus likes a rat. Oh Lord forgive me, I didn't mean to say that. I had my suspicions though, about who Ernest really was. Had a little ratty look to 'is own face did he, made me love 'im all the more, it did. Not like his other two, ratty faces and all. Can't find not a thing in them to love. I knows we is all God's children, but no siree, not them two. Nasty pieces of work, if ever there was.

They tormented our poor little Ernest from the git go. No wonder he was so keen on spending his time downstairs with the likes of us. What with putting critters of all sorts in his bed and hiding his one drawer of clothes so Ernest had to come down in just his small clothes on more than one occasion. He'd just come on in to the breakfast room and sit meekly down, not looking at a soul. His little face all red. Those nasty…, God forgive me.

What clothes he did have were nothing special anyway, old and torn up more like. I says to the master one evening, "Ernest, the little tyke, sure could use some different clothes, if you don't mind my saying so."

"I do mind you saying so" he said as he glared at me, but I wasn't backing down, not when it was for our poor little Ernest.

"I was thinking, mighn't there be some older things of the young master's he could have? I wouldn't mind doing a bit of altering for him." I hurried in a rush to get out.

"What, give him hand me downs?" he spat. Then that look came over his face, the cheap bas… well, Oh Lord forgive me, but it's God's honest truth. "That's a splendid idea, Mrs. Bakerson (I's aint married but cooks and housekeepers is always called by Mrs.). Ernest is looking a little worn around the edges these days. Go on up to the attic and see what you can find."

Afterwards, when I gave them to Ernest his little ratty face lit up like it was Christmastime morn come again. I had to run out of the room to hide my wet eyes. Had no one ever given that wonderful little boy a gift before? I determined then and there that as long as he was in this house, and I had a breath in my body, our poor little Ernest was gonna have the best I could beg borrow or steal for him. Lord forgive me if it ain't so.

But I failed him.

Oh, I tried to protect him from them. Our poor little Ernest, bless his small heart, he wanted to keep every critter for a pet he found in his bed or in his shoes. Wouldn't harm the hair on a fly's head, no siree. He was forever asking for boxes and food for the poor creatures. Frogs, spiders, centipedes, it made no difference to Ernest, they was all loved. I finally convinced him they'd be much happier outside in the Lord's free world, but as he was as near to tears as I'd ever seen 'im, so I allowed he could keep his two favorite ones. He was so happy. He chose a lumpy old frog and a bat that couldn't fly, of all things. They were cared for and loved better than anyone else upstairs ever was. He even named the bat Mrs. Bakerson. When I found that out I cried for an hour. There it was written on the outside of the box in his little, shaky scrawl. I found it when I was cleaning out his things.

Ernest wasn't allowed any learning, not like the other two with their tutors three days a week. When I found that out, I set our poor little Ernest up right outside the open door in a chair to listen in on the lessons. Old Mr. started to object but I just glared at him and he backed down, but he didn't look on me all that friendly after that. Ask me if I cared. The other two sneered at Ernest when they found out, but it didn't faze our poor little Ernest none. I don't think his pure heart understood the concept of hate, but that is sure what I was seeing.

I made sure Ernest had everything I could give him. I cooked only his favorite foods and made only his favorite desserts. When the other two complained, "what, roast chicken, again" I just smiled and shrugged. "You don't have to eat it", I would mumble to them, so the Old Mr. couldn't hear. Those two took to glaring at me too after that.

It was when Christmas time, that most blessed of days, came around for real that the straw broke the camel's back, as they say in India, I suppose. Oh, there were many presents under the tree in the parlor that year. All shapes and sizes all brightly wrapped in store bought paper and ribbons and bows. But not a one for our poor little Ernest. I was livid! I felt a rage and a sorrow I have never felt and let me tell you with my hand to God, my life was never very easy neither. But this, this was unforgiveable in my mind. Imagine our poor little Ernest running downstairs Christmas morning to nothing. It was probably like every previous Christmas I reckon.

Well not this time. I marched into the old Mr's study, I didn't even knock now mind you, and when he looked up at me from his tying his infernal fishing flys, (what a crazy thing for a growd man to do). He was first surprised then mad.

"What is the meaning of this"? he bellowed.

It was then I noticed the half-filled whiskey decanter and empty glass by his elbow. I have to say I was momentarily taken back with wondering if this shouldn't wait till morning. *But No,* I thought, *Christmas is in two days' time and our poor little Ernest deserved better.*

"There aint be one gif under that tree for our poor little Ernest." I said.

That stopped the old coot for a second. Not what he was expecting I'm guessing.

"What?" he asked with a dangerous glint in his eyes. I clutched my cross a little tighter and I says clear as I could, "Ernest deserves gifts on Christmastime Morn too just like your others."

He wasn't no stupid man. He got right to understanding what I was saying.

"Ernest isn't mine," he stammered. "He is in my foster care that is all. His poor mother was a distant friend of the family, that's all."

Sounded rehearsed to me, and that ratty look tells me different, but I didn't say so. "That's as it is, but what about Christmastime morning then? What about Ernest's gifts?" I insisted

He was clearly flummoxed. "I didn't even think..." something on my face must have told him I wasn't a believer. "I'm sorry I didn't think of it." He just sat there looking a little dejected. Maybe there was a glimmer of hope for this man. "I give him a warm bed, and good food, and, well...you don't cook *my* favorites I noticed."

"That boy need someone to love him," I said.

"Bah, it's too late now, no one is going into town before Christmas" and with that he turned back to his flies.

It wasn't too late, I saw plenty of things up in that attic our poor little Ernest would love. I wasn't askin no permission either, the good Lord forgive me. I myself had already knitted him a sweater, the poor thing always looked so cold, but I had nothing nice to wrap it in. It was jus then I knew nothing would ever be better for our poor, little Ernest, but in my heart, I knew there was one thing our poor little Ernest needed.

When Christmastime Morning came, Ernest was straight down the stairs and into the parlor and even the other two didn't harass him too much on this day. They was all laughing and jolly. The other two tore through the gifts, but our poor little Ernest just sat on the edge of the sofa, with his legs swinging with hope and dejection battling across his face. The old Mr. was down there too, and when one or the other started to be nasty to Ernest, a quick look from him put an end to it, for that I blessed him.

Finally, they tossed his presents back to him and our poor little Ernest looked on with what I could only say was disbelief. He had a pile of presents like he had never, ever seen or expected. They wasn't all wrapped up fancy like the others, but they was his. I'd never seen our poor little Ernest so happy either 'fore or after. If I had been worried about the Old Mr.'s reaction when he saw where our poor little Ernest's gifts had come from, I needn't had bothered. As he left the Parlor for the breakfast room, he looked back at me and gave me a little nod of his head. But I knew the time had come.

A couple of weeks later, when they all were back to their usual mean and nasty selves, it happened. As our poor little Ernest sat alone at the big table, I brung him his dessert fore that night, A big fresh juicy peach, I had saved out specially for him. Ernest loved peaches, and they could be hard to come by in the winter, fresh ones anyways.

Our poor little Ernest left us that night. But they never did say how it happened, 'cept he choked on his peach. I assume the old Mr. thought one of his offspring had done it and wanted it kept shushed up. It was never spoke about again.

Father come closer to my bed. It's time I confessed and sought God's forgiveness, afore I leave this world for my judgment. I poisoned our poor little Ernest's peach that night. A soul as pure and as good as his has no place on this cruel mean earth. Things were never gonna be better for that poor boy, so I sent him back to God.

The End.

FANNY

Fanny dreaded what was about to happen. It had been promised, or threatened depending on your perspective, that Fanny was to be sent to the country for the summer. New Orleans was just fine to Fanny, she loved the hustle and bustle, loved her house and her room, loved her pet cat, Mabel, who she rescued from the gutter two years ago. She loved her best friends, Sally-Ann and Jacob, who lived down the street. Loved the parks and the water, and well, everything.

"Why?" she screamed at her Mama and Papa, tears threatening to overwhelm her quivering face, when they told her with smiles on their faces. It was about the worse thing Fanny could imagine. Why did her parents hate her so? Life was so unfair!

Her parents imagined many different types of reactions from Fanny, most of them included happiness and joy, maybe indifference, but not these tears and shouting. Momentarily they doubted their decision. Fanny's parents were having, a few marital difficulties this year, things a young girl Fanny's age didn't need to worry about. They had felt it would be best if Fanny went to visit her cousins for the summer while they rekindled their love, if they could. They loved Fanny with all their hearts, as parents usually do, so this tantrum was not sitting well with the guilt they were already feeling.

Had Fanny known they were already feeling uncomfortably guilty about sending her away, she may have been able to win the day with some judicious pleading, crying and recriminations, i.e. "You hate me or you wouldn't make me go!" kinds of things, and maybe a couple of "please, please's". Alas, after the initial outburst, Fanny could only sniffle and look dejected, with her head down and her hands being wrung.

"Oh honey", this was her father kneeling down and lifting her chin up with one finger, "you love your cousins. Remember how much fun you had with them last year when they came for Christmas?"

Sniffle, "yes" in that little Fanny voice. Mostly that was because here, Fanny was queen of the house and got to show them all her great things and her great city. *Who can say what it'll be like there*, she thought.

"And don't you love Aunt Mable too? You named the cat after her after all," her mother reasoned. Actually at the time, Fanny had momentarily forgot her Aunt's name was also Mable. She was trying to name the cat Marble after the swirl of colors, but it didn't come out right. Fanny did love Aunt Mable, but thought she smelled funny.

"She smells funny," Fanny sniffed.

Her mother smiled, holding back a laugh. "Now you know it's just the ointment she uses for her arthritis. Don't you want to go to see your cousins and aunt and uncle and you'll do all sorts of fun things, we promise."

Fanny was still unconvinced but was at least peering up at her parent's faces now from under her golden curls, just a twinkle of a lone tear caught in her lashes.

"I'll tell you what," her father said to her with a wink, his mustachioed lips turning up in a smile, "we will talk on the phone every day and if you really don't like it, you can come home immediately. How about that eh?"

So finally, Fanny concurred and that is how she ended up at her uncle's in the country for the summer, with her cousins.

And then tragedy struck.

Just a week after Fanny's arrival at the farm, Fanny's cousin Jimmy fell down and broke his leg. The three cousins, Fanny, Melissa and the aforementioned Jimmy were running through a nearby field when Fanny slipped and fell, stirring up a swarm of...

"Bees!" Fanny screamed, hopping up and running willy-nilly back toward the house, the peaked roof of which they could just see over the hill. Jimmy hated bees, being stung two summers ago multiple times, so he was particularly panicked. When Jimmy turned to escape the field and what was sure to be a huge swarm of nasty bees, he twisted his ankle, fell on a rock and broke his leg.

Turns out it wasn't bees Fanny had stirred up, but crickets, which in her defense, could hop pretty high when disturbed. They didn't sting or do much of anything else except make noise. How was a city girl to know?

Aunt Mable came a-running at all the commotion, rubbing her hands on her substantial apron, stray locks of hair streaming behind her after escaping her bun, tsk, tsking the whole way.

After the doctor fixed Jimmy up in a cast, which Fanny thought was cool looking, mostly because they were able to write on it, the three cousins were flummoxed about what to do. Jimmy couldn't go outside, being ensconced on the living room sofa for at least for a week the doc said. And Jimmy had promised, promised Fanny to show her the swamp with the gators and the sasquash. Now it'll be forever before she could go! This summer, which was gonna be so great, now is ruined! Life is so unfair, Fanny desperately felt. Forgetting that just a little more than a week gone by she would have done anything other than come here in the first place.

Aunt Mable came to the rescue. She came into the living room where all three kids dejectedly sat, bemoaning the unfairness of life, though for different reasons, with a big, enormous pile of brightly colored boxes in her large arms.

"Here you go sweeties, this will keep you having fun," She said.

"What is it" Fanny asked, with her eyes big and round looking at the pile now sitting on the coffee table. (Now here's a strange thing for a young girl, just as a side point, Fanny had never seen a puzzle before, but I don't know why.)

"Why they're puzzles, girl," Aunt Mable said, the same time Melissa said, "puzzles, silly!"

"Here, clear the rest of this stuff off the table", She told the kids, with her big arm sweeping clear the usual things coffee tables collect, magazines and what not, onto the floor. All three kids squealed with the unusualness of it all. "You three do them right here" and upon smelling something maybe just getting a tad overcooked in the kitchen, said to her own two as she turned to go, "Show your little cousin how to do 'em".

Turns out, Fanny loved the puzzles. The kids put together puzzles day and night, hardly wanting to stop to eat or sleep. "I gotta pee, don't do anymore till I get back" one or the other of them would be heard to exclaim now and again while running or hobbling out of the livingroom.

Here was a large ship on the ocean, here was a red barn in a field with wild flowers, and here was a range of snowcapped mountains, probably from somewhere far away, Fanny imagined. In fact, the kid's imaginations ran away that week of summer, with all the exotic places and things pictured on those puzzles.

However, no matter how much you like puzzles and no matter your age it is hard to stay interested after about a week. Fortunately, when the doc came back, he declared Jimmy could be up and about if he used the crutches and was careful.

Finally, the whole world of exploration was back open before the three of them.

"Now can we go see the gators and the sasquash?" Fanny whispered to Jimmy one evening after supper, while they were alone in the living room. For this is all Fanny was thinking about, in her secret places. Imagine the story she will have to tell Sally-Ann and Jacob about the gator and the sasquash. They will be so jealous!

"I don't know" Jimmy said with uncertainty lining his face. It might be hard on crutches he was thinking. The doc said not to get the leg wet, even though the swamp wasn't more than two feet deep in most places, and to be honest he never had seen a gator, never mind a sasquatch only frogs and leeches mostly. "We'll have to wait and see."

Every child in history that ever was or ever will be knows the meaning of the words "We'll have to wait and see," it means no. Again, the unfairness of life struck Fanny to the core. Her lips quivered and she fought back tears. She wanted more than anything ever to see the gators and the sasquash, especially the sasquash.

"Maybe Missy, (that's what Fanny called her cousin Melissa) could take me?" A little hope creeping into her voice. But Jimmy remained incredulous.

"She don't know where it is" he said, "plus she's scared of it, all girls are," he threw in as an extra deterrent.

"I am not," Melissa, who had been eavesdropping demanded with hands on hips, little chin jutting out, coming from around the door. "And I do know where it is!"

"Where then? Missy know it all," Jimmy demanded, tauntingly.

Now up to this point, it should be noted that the kids got along remarkably well. But a week cooped up inside had apparently taken its toll. Melissa stuck her tongue out at her brother. "It's behind the barn, over that way," she waved uncertainly in some direction.

"Ha, ha," Jimmy laughed, making Melissa angry "You'll never find it."

If only he had been right. Strangely, Fanny's death by leech brought her parents closer together than ever, so that part worked out anyway.

The End.

GEORGE

Barbara herself was small, barely reaching a respectable five feet tall, and that with heels on! She was often being mistaken for a young girl even into her twenties. She longed for the day when she might have a little grey in her hair, so people would stop calling her 'missy' and 'young miss'.

After college, on job interviews she was often first met with silence as people attempted to size her up as it were, no pun intended. In line at the pharmacy or hardware store, she was often overlooked. Those clerks that noticed her at all assumed she was somebody's daughter. She would often joke with friends, "at the end of the world, if God spares only the children, he may overlook me." And don't think getting into a bar or nightclub wasn't just hysterical.

Once she became pregnant though, people didn't know what to think of Barbara's age. She certainly didn't look old enough to have a child, but these days, who knows?

When George was born he was tiny, barely four pounds. Being three weeks early hadn't helped out any either. Why, he was barely knee-high to a grasshopper, as the saying goes. But he had full sized lungs, and did they work! George was a terribly loud baby, constantly wailing and snotting. The poor thing barely slept, at least that's how it felt to Barbara and likewise Barbara felt as if she barely slept. She picked him up, he cried. She put him down, he cried. She fed him, he cried. She didn't feed him, he cried. She bathed him, well you get it, he cried and cried and cried. If any new mother had thoughts of infanticide, it couldn't have been for a more compelling reason.

Barbara was ecstatic to flee back to work, like some daily migratory bird.

There was only one issue. George still cried. He cried when around his father. He cried when around his grandparents, aunts, uncles and cousins. George cried for years, no matter what you did for him, to him or fed him or gave him to play with or to cuddle. Even the cat ran away and the faithful hound was seriously considering its options.

Finally, when George turned four, it was decided professional help was called for. If ever a family needed a Mary Poppins or a Nanny McPhee, this was it.

What, or should I say whom, they got instead was Cindy.

Cindy was a non-descript, marginally intelligent, kind of dull young lady who had just happened to be stood up at the altar. With her hopes of marriage dashed and her parents anxious to have her move on (and out), Cindy became George's live-in nanny. They call them Au Pair's today though because, well, the term 'nanny' is so old-fashioned. Cindy didn't actually like children but sensing some last chance of a life away from her parent's disappointed eyes, she managed to convey at least an interest in the little things. It helped that Barbara was desperate.

At first, George didn't take to this newcomer, so he... you guessed it, cried. Morning, noon and night. He cried when Cindy looked at him. He cried when she didn't. He cried when Cindy dressed him, fed him, took him outside, or laid him down for a nap. Now thankfully Cindy wasn't too imaginative, or she may have seen a few ways to end this infernal crying and wouldn't have been the first Au Pair to do it.

After about a year of this, what did happen though, is that Cindy stumbled onto a solution. In a pure move of desperation (it took a lot to get one of Cindy's limits to feel something as strong as desperation), she invented a game for George.

Hide and Seek.

Now you and I both know, Hide and Seek was invented when the first Cavemom forced her Cavekids under the old animal skins in the back of the cave when their Cavedad had that special gleam in his eyes.

"Grunt grunt grunt," (go hide under the skins, I'll find you later) she would say and off they would go.

For Cindy and George, it happened was like this:

George dropped his pacifier behind the couch. I know, he was now five but the pacifier barely had time to be in his mouth anyway, what with all the crying. Cindy set George down on the floor, wiped some snot off her blouse, slightly slid the couch out from the wall and disappeared behind it.

George immediately stopped crying. Startled by this turn of events, Cindy immediately poked her head back up to see if George had suddenly passed away or been abducted by aliens. Upon seeing Cindy's disembodied head, he giggled. Cindy popped back down. George outright laughed, while standing up and walking closer to the back of the couch, snot drooling down his nose and onto his chin the whole way. "I found you," George said laughing, when he peered fully behind the sofa. That may have been the first time George ever managed to string two or more words together not interrupted by tearful crying.

Cindy suspected she was onto something. That whole day, Cindy hid behind things and George came and found her, laughing. That night George slept so soundly and quietly, his parents got no sleep at all for the seventeen times they got up to check and see if he was still breathing.

George became an expert finder. No matter where Cindy hid, George could find her. In the closet in his parent's bedroom, no problem, under the dining room table, Gotcha! In the kitchen pantry, Ah-ha; laughing the whole time. Was that the new cat going into the litter box? George was there poking his head in to find her also. Sadly, she ran away as well.

Now poor simple Cindy was getting a little tired. After all, no matter how big the house was, there were only so many places to hide, but an idea did occur to her, finally.

"George, now you hide, and I will find you."

George's eyes became wide, his lower lip started to quiver, then he smiled. "Okay", and off he skedaddled. Now remember, George was small. He could fit into and hide in places no normal child of five or even three could. Though Cindy did have to insist the oven and inside the back of the commode was off limits. Cindy spent all day trying to find George who turned out to be quite a creative little fellow.

In the hat box under his parent's bed? Cindy never did find him, and he eventually ran off to bed, happy as a lark. Behind the books on one of his Father's bookcases? Finally, he came out to happily eat dinner. In the cookie jar, on the high shelf? Don't be silly, he wasn't that small.

Cindy may have slowed down in her searches for George and who could blame her? George was perfectly happy hiding for two or three hours curled up behind the winter coats, muffling his giggles.

It was a happy and quiet time in the house with only George's laughter or snores indicating his presence.

Until the fateful day *they* came.

Barbara decided it was time for new furniture, the old having been unceremoniously sprayed with George's snot and tears for the last five years. Like all socially conscious and respectable families, Barbara donated the old stuff to charity. The overall'd men came and off they carted all the old living room furniture, leaving the room bare except for the big old rug on the floor ready for the new furnishings. All the while George was still playing Hide and Seek. The absence of furniture couldn't stop him.

Sadly Cindy, who may have been fantasizing about a particularly handsome and muscular moving man didn't think to look for George until bedtime.

The lump under the rug was no longer giggling, but no longer crying either.

The End.

Hector

The school was one of those small, under-funded country institutions where every teacher and administrator knew your entire family. They knew everything every older sibling, every cousin, and in some cases even, parents when they went there did for good or for bad. By the time you managed to go, they each already had an opinion, an expectation of what you would be like and what you would do, based purely on family history. All small country schools were the same, especially these in the English countryside where family upbringing accounted for everything. "Well, look at the parents (or aunt or brother), what do you expect?" Someone would knowingly say. Little or no consideration was given to individuality.

Of course, in general this rule only applied to the bad. If you somehow managed to excel in some area beyond your family history, say sports or academics, the general rule of thumb was that it was accomplished despite your family. Most probably a direct result of the (imaginary) extra care and concern shown to you from these very teachers and/or administrators. "I thought I saw something different about *her*," meaning to differentiate you from your bad familial influences. Then your children, should they be unfortunate enough to go there also, had the extra burden of being expected to do special things too.

Hector had it even worse. Imagine being the only Latino child in this quaint English seaside village school. The teachers had no family history to pull apart to account for Hector's bad grades, disciplinarian problems, excellent sports achievements or whatever. They only had every single thing they had ever seen on TV or in the movies or heard about the entire Latino culture and peoples to judge Hector by. It was a heavy burden to bear for a young man of barely nine years old.

Hector's parents ended up here purely by a series of accidental events. It was quite amusing actually, except possibly to Hector's family, but that is a story for another time. Suffice it to say, no one in Hector's family wanted to be there among the English country snobs.

Hector had a tough time of it.

"Of course he got into a fight, they're a hot blooded people," one might over hear in the teachers' lounge. Forget that the real reason was that several older boys were bullying a younger kid and Hector stood up to his defense. And after being called several choice insults pertaining to his parentage and culture, had no choice but to fight.

Or, "of course his homework wasn't completed, they are lazy by nature." Forget that Hector was busy helping to care for his elderly and ailing grandmother all evening while his parents were again kept overtime at work to make up for some imagined lack of work ethic. "Maria, clean the dining room again, please. Really you could do so much better if you just tried." Or to his father, "Some of the men are complaining they can't understand your directions, you are going to have to go through it all and make sure it was done right."

When Hector failed to grasp the reason for all the kings and queens and wars and petty family rivalries that tore England apart for so many years hundreds of years ago, it was said, "what do you expect, he isn't from a refined culture like ours they barely have a government."

When certain drugs started rearing their ugly faces in town, heads were turned and behind empty hands it was whispered to one another, "you know where that came from."

Not surprisingly, like many a marginalized young person judged only on skin tone, Hector began to feel like he had something to prove.

Hector's parents worried about him. They knew if they were having a tough time acclimating, or being accepted for themselves, he was having a terrible time. Kids his age are so cruel and rarely does teacher interference help. Hector did his best to ignore the taunts and the ignorance of his classmates. He felt that if he excelled at classwork or at athletics, he could be accepted. At his age, acceptance is important, but down inside Hector knew it would be a mistake to do so at the cost of his heritage.

When the date of a traditional Latino holiday was approaching, Hector asked for permission to set up a little display of his native land's traditional culture on a table in the library, which he would man all day to answer questions. Also, his teacher could give him extra credit for the extra work (two birds, one stone).

"Would that be appropriate," several of them twittered in the teachers' lounge. "It's just one table," a more open-minded member of staff commented. "But don't we want him to fit in more, not stand out," asked the old curmudgeon who taught music. "They want to live here, they should at least try to be English." And on and on, many voices of prejudice arguing against the few of reason.

Finally, as the day approached to where it would almost be too late to get it done, the answer came down: "Maybe next year, thank you for the nice idea though."

Hector was disappointed but he wasn't finished. He knew the road to his peers' acceptance wasn't his conforming to them, his skin will always be darker. It was them liking and respecting him as he was.

Hector started inviting his classmates to his home for meals, homework or just fun. Some came, some did not. All who came seem friendly enough and enjoyed themselves. Hector's parents were glad to see he was making friends here, finally. However, at school little changed. The kids Hector thought he was reaching were still too encumbered by peer pressure, fear or shame to admit their friendships with him.

Some of these kids' fathers worked for Hector's father, who was a supervisor at the factory. In Hector's mind they should be less inclined to prejudice, not more. In actuality, Hector's family was one of the better off in this little village, having a two-income family. But the fact that a Latino was placed above them, just made the fathers more unreasonable and thus the kids, no matter how well deserved the placement. In contrast, the families Hector's mom worked for as a maid, those that had kids were nicer to Hector, in a condescending kind of way.

Smarter and older people than Hector didn't understand the psychology that made this so, so how could Hector?

Nearing the end of the school year in an atypical warm and sunny month, Hector stumbled upon an idea. Part of the reason his family ended up here, he knew from his parents, shall we say, *discussions*, was due to a cousin of his fathers who worked at the embassy in London. Hector of course has been in the embassy, and it was great. Built and decorated in the style of his country, with courtyards and traditional gardens, the embassy boasted a museum with a film detailing the shared history, mutual respect and good works they and the English people had accomplished not only in both nations but around the globe.

Hector doubted he could bring the embassy to them, but his plan was to bring them to the embassy. After all, his class took field trips for all sorts of stupid reasons. They went to a goat farm to see the goats. They went to a veterinarian's office to see the vet work. They went to a small archeology dig to see bits of dug up old stone. It was boring, mundane stuff in Hector's mind.

He set about arranging it right away.

"Dad, my class wants to take a field trip to the embassy. How do I do it?" Forget that his class knew nothing about it, yet. Proudly, his dad called his cousin who was happy to make the arrangements.

Hector ran to school the whole way the next morning with the news for the administrator.

"Whoa, there Hector, I'm not sure we can just send your whole class off to London for the day, even if the ambassador invited you. I'm sure it's a great idea, but I'm not sure it's in the budget. Maybe next year," dismissing Hector with what he hoped was a genial smile.

They all had a good talking over this latest idea of Hector's in the teachers' lounge that lunchtime. "Imagine, going to London, just to see some buildings with a courtyard." "Actually, I hear the gardens there are beautiful, I'd love to go", was fairly drowned out with the negatives, "too far, not safe, too costly." What they all meant was, "too Latino."

It just so happened, Hector's father's cousin came visiting that evening. The phone call reminding him it had been too long since he saw the family. He was there when Hector arrived home from school.

"So, Hector" after all the hugs and kisses, "is your class excited about coming to the embassy?"

Hector was crestfallen, battling tears. "The administrator says we can't. The school can't afford it."

Hector's father and his father's cousin exchanged a knowing look. "I'll take care of it, leave it all to me, eh, Hector?"

The next day the ambassador *himself* called the school administrator, not only inviting Hector's class to the embassy for a day, but also offering to pay for the whole trip, out of the cultural budget. When the administrator still tried to object, the ambassador offered to call the central supervisor's office, "if it would help". The trip was scheduled for the next Thursday and permission slips were sent out forthwith.

The bus picked up Hector's class at 8:00 am for the one-and-a-half-hour trip into London. The kids were all very excited, and the two teachers as well, though they tried to hide it. Imagine an invitation from the ambassador himself. They felt puffed up with their own importance.

All the kids were encouraged to wear their best school uniforms and Hector was similarly decked out in his school hat, jacket and tie. Upon arrival in London, the bus disgorged the excited and noisome flock of children squarely in front of the embassy's main gates. The two teachers present were getting flustered getting them all under control, especially the curmudgeonly old music teacher. As the bus pulled away to park in a lot about a block and a half away, she realized she left her purse under her seat with the pills she had to take with her lunch.

"Oh my," she exclaimed. "My purse is still on the bus."

"I'll go get it," said the other teacher, "it's not far." But the old music teacher felt worried about herding all these troublesome children herself.

"No, we have all these children to look after," and spying Hector listening said "Hector, be a dear would you and run to the bus driver and get my purse, you know where the bus is, don't you?"

Well, he didn't. But what nine-year-old boy would admit ignorance? He saw the bus went that way and heard it was only a block and a half. "Sure thing," being ever ready to please. "I'll be back in a jiffy." And off he went.

Now we will never know if the thug was trying to kidnap Hector for ransom, mistaking him for some wealthy family's child, or if poor Hector was just in the wrong place at the wrong time perhaps seeing something he shouldn't of. However it all transpired, Hector didn't make it home that day from London, or any day after.

The End

IDA

Ivy and her twin sister Ida believe in Mermaids (with a capital 'M'). They believe in Mermaids with their whole hearts. Of course, they also believe in the Tooth Fairy, the Easter Bunny and all sorts of other fantastical creatures and beings. Belief isn't the problem.

Ivy and Ida don't want to be the Easter Bunny. They want to be Mermaids.

"Isn't that just so adorable", you might think, as did Ivy and Ida's Aunt Louise, upon first hearing about it.

Now Aunt Louise is a wonderful person, forever happy to be doing things for her family and her neighbors. Baking, sewing, cooking and what not, Aunt Louise is a giver if ever there was one.

At first Ivy and Ida's parents saw no harm with their girls' infatuation with Mermaids. They were just the age, after all. Mermaids and unicorns one day, boys the next. Or so they thought (Ivy and Ida didn't actually like unicorns or boys, not yet anyway).

In the beginning, they were happy to buy Ivy and Ida all sorts of Mermaid themed stuff, Mermaid pillows, Mermaid coloring books and story books about Mermaids, Mermaid shaped pancakes, you get the picture. But no matter how much Mermaid paraphernalia Ivy and Ida got, the more it seemed they wanted.

When Ivy and Ida's teacher (they were in the same class) sent a note home to their parents asking to speak with them they didn't give it any special thought. Teachers speak to parents, it's how it works.

When Ivy and Ida's teacher showed their parents some Mermaid drawings Ivy and Ida had done, two thoughts immediately crossed their minds. *Our kids are really good little artists* and *what the hell?*

The drawings were graphic. A pair of Mermaids were wooing sailors to their violent deaths. A pair of Mermaids were ruling an underwater world. A pair of Mermaids who were copulating with humans. The most disturbing part, the absolutely most terrifying part, for Ivy and Ida's parents was the Mermaids in the drawings had Ivy's and Ida's face.

The teacher felt at a loss. She was young and inexperienced and her "How to be a Teacher for Dummies" book had no relevant advice. "Are the children subjected to violence at home", she asked. "Of course not", the parents truthfully answered. "Is there some traumatic childhood event that they are repressing", she asked. "Of course not", the parents truthfully answered. "Are they being bullied by someone", the teacher asked. "Of course not", the parents truthfully answered. The teacher was better than she gave herself credit for. She asked all the right questions, but unfortunately there seemed to be no good answer to the Ivy and Ida Mermaid dilemma.

Back at home all the Mermaid stuff went into the trash and was carted off to the dump. The Mermaid pillows? No more. The Mermaid posters? Good-bye. The Mermaid bedspreads, lamp shades and Mermaid pancakes? Adios. The Mermaid books? Burnt to ash that blew away on the wind.

When Ivy and Ida came home that day they discovered they were suddenly and inexplicably Mermaidless.

This was the first part of the plan. The rest, well it was decided that Ivy and Ida should spend some time apart, summer vacation was coming up and each individually should be given their parents' undivided attention and introduced to some more appropriate things.

Upon hearing about her little darling's Mermaidal instability, naturally Aunt Louise offered to help.

"What those girls need is a good old-fashioned summer on the farm." And so, it was decided.

For two weeks each Ivy and Ida would go separately to Aunt Louise's and one of their parents would go with them while the other stayed at home with the non-farm visiting sibling.

Work schedules were arranged, travel plans made. Four weeks to introduce Ivy and Ida, independent of each other, to other, more appropriate interests.

It was decided by chance that Ivy would go first. She would be the first of the pair to visit Aunt Louise that summer with their mother. Ida would stay at home with their father, and then visit Aunt Louise after Ivy returned.

If it hadn't been for the catfish, the plan may have been a success.

Normally, you'd expect the separation of two close siblings to be traumatic, at least at the start, especially more so for identical twins. But Ivy and Ida didn't mind being separated. They both loved and looked forward to seeing Aunt Louise. The fact that the woman never stopped baking may also have been a factor.

The first two weeks it seemed, went great.

Ida's time was spent doing and learning about all the things her father thought would interest a girl her age. One day they went bowling, one day they went to a ball game, one day they went to the zoo, one day they saw a princess movie, one day they went to a car show and one day they attempted to cook dinner, practically burning down the house, rolling with laughter. Ida loved spending this special time with her dad, but deep down, she never forgot she was a Mermaid queen.

Ivy though was swayed by all the new and interesting things shown her. Ivy and her mother went for country hikes and they swam in the still waters of the small, nearby lake. Ivy learned how to use and apply make-up and learned how to bake, possibly being the only girl her age who could bake a perfect cheesecake, Aunt Louise's specialty. Ivy also saw the new princess movie and thought she might like to be a princess one day, all thoughts of being a Mermaid queen pushed slowly from her mind. The two weeks fairly flew past.

Then the switch came. Only for one day would Ivy and Ida be together at home. After the explanations of all the things done and the exclamations of wonder over Ivy's cheesecakes (of which there were plenty, cheesecakes I mean. They can be frozen you know), the commiseration over Ida's blisters, (learning how to play golf) and after the joy of being reunited, Ivy and Ida found themselves alone together in their room, their parents seeking some together time for themselves.

"Let's play Mermaid queens" Ida said. "You can be Queen Marta," one of their favorite Mermaid characters.

"Nah, I want to show you how to put on lipstick" Ivy replied. "Here, do you want red or pink?" pulling two partially squashed lipsticks out of her new, little purse. And though the lipsticks did intrigue Ida, she was concerned over her sister's lack of Mermaidal interest.

"You don't want to be Queen Marta?" she inquired. Everyone wanted to be Queen Marta.

"Mermaids are silly, they aren't real," Ivy simply replied while gazing in the mirror, not understanding the effect her words would have on Ida.

Ida was in shock and remained so for the whole trip to Aunt Louise's farm, where she now did not want to go. Something obviously happened to Ivy there, something (shudder) sinister, she believed.

Aunt Louise was glad to see Ida, whom she loved just as much as Ivy. Aunt Louise wanted to teach Ida how to bake, *maybe a nice berry pie*, she thought. Ida's mother and her Aunt Louise tried all the things with Ida they had tried with Ivy, but to no avail. Ida seemed to be lost in her mind. Oh, she was polite enough, and feigned interest in things, but Ida was determined to get to the bottom of the Ivy mystery.

Near the middle of the second week, the answer presented itself to Ida.

One of Aunt Louise's old and garrulous neighbors stopped by, just to talk (while having a big plate full of cheesecake, mind you). During this fairly boring adult conversation around the kitchen table, Ida heard the magic words, "that dang ol' great big granddaddy catfish." Apparently, several years ago, as no doubt Aunt Louise had heard many times, the neighbor had almost hooked himself a big 'ol catfish, the biggest in the county. Now supposedly, this granddaddy catfish taunts the old man at every opportunity.

"Where is this?" Ida interrupted, not really having been listening.

"Why right here in your Aunt Louise's little lake, honey", he answered, brushing crumbs of cheesecake from off his overalls.

Ida now knew for a certainty what had happened to Ivy. Many years ago in some undisclosed location, Queen Marta's younger sister Taurine had been abducted by the King Under the Water, according to a story they had read. Upon finding this out, Queen Marta cursed the King to be forever in the form of a great big catfish, who was just too wily to ever be caught.

This catfish, right here in Aunt Louise's pond, must be the very one. The King Under the Water. He must have stolen the real Ivy and is keeping her in one of his dark underwater caves so talked about in the story, Ida knew now for a certainty.
She considered telling the adults, but after looking around at them thought it best to handle it herself. Adults were unpredictable.

That next morning early, just as the eastern sky was lightning and the mist was slowly lifting off the lake, Ida stole out of the house still in her nightgown and ran down to the lake to rescue her sister Ivy's true self from the King Under the Water. The early morning dew was wet and cool on her bare feet.

The little boat was easy to push out onto the still lake and climb into. Ida was determined to search all day for the underwater cave, if she had to. She searched and searched, at least until the cold dark water stole the breath from her one last time.

 She never did find that wily old catfish.

The End.

JAMES

The pastor at the Abiding Savior Lutheran church in Verona, Wisconsin, Pastor Jensen, was partial to enjoying a glass or two of Lakka every evening after supper. Lakka is the traditional alcoholic drink of his forebears from Finland, crafted out of cloudberries. Cloudberries resemble very, very pale black-eyed peas, but grow on bushes like blueberries, way up north in the Scandinavian countries. I guess God or Odin or whomever, figured if you managed to trek all the way up there, or somehow managed to eke out an actual living just consuming codfish, you deserved a treat. Viola, the cloudberry.

Pastor Jensen was an aging, balding, over-weight celibate who chose to dedicate his life to God after the very narrow escape of almost marrying his high school interest, Brigitte Andersen, who at the time was already balding and over-weight. For many years, Father Jensen used to thank God profusely whenever he encountered his erstwhile girlfriend at church or community functions (something that happens quite often), for she has gotten balder and heavier with the passing years.

Neither of them had ever left Verona for very long. Pastor Jensen to go to Seminary, and one year of service abroad, and young Brigitte to one year of university in Milwaukee where she chanced to not only attach herself to another local boy, the unfortunate and apparently desperate, Harold Lindberg, by some unlikely means, but also come home pregnant. It wasn't long before she was married in the very church where the good Father Jensen now serves though scandalously, the pastor at the time wouldn't allow her to wear white, a tradition that has fallen to the wayside. It didn't keep the young Brigitte from radiating happiness on her entire waddle down the aisle.

Maybe, some of the older generation in the congregation assume, Harold and Brigitte's union was actually one of love and mutual respect, rather than desperation and shame. After all, they stayed married for thirty-five years, through three children, until Harold's untimely death in an ice fishing accident and seemed if not exactly happy, at least content for most of it.

The good Pastor Jensen, as was the habit in the area, lived in a small stone house attached to the rear of the small stone church in which he served his small congregation of faithful. The house having been vacated many years earlier upon the death of Father Jensen's predecessor and mentor in the faith, who interestingly also enjoyed the occasional glass of Lakka.

Brigitte Andersen, now Brigitte Lindberg these many long years, as mentioned earlier, had three children. Two of them couldn't wait to leave Verona as soon as possible, both settling in somewhat warmer climes. This story isn't about them, so forget about them. The youngest, however stayed and married the very pretty, if somewhat dimwitted, high school basketball star, James 'Jimmy' Bronson, who after graduation worked in his father's garage fixing automobiles (a more lucrative business than you might imagine). They also had three children, the youngest, being the only boy, was named James, jr.

Now young James loved his grandmother Brigitte. He didn't care that she was fat and bald. In young James' eyes, she was a kind, warm, soft, cuddly and loving grandmother. Maybe that was some of what Harold saw in her? At any rate, the two were almost inseparable. As they lived on the same street, much to Jimmy's dismay at times, they were seemingly attached at the hip. Wherever Brigitte went, there was young James.

Now the fact that Brigitte was a founding member of the Abiding Savior Lutheran Church Women's Auxiliary meant Brigitte was very involved with the church and the community. If she ever felt uncomfortable seeing Pastor Jensen so often, the man she almost married, or in fact if she even ever thought about it, she gave no indication. It seems of the pair, only Pastor Jensen had that particular hang-up.

This then, is how James came to know Pastor Jensen so well. Of course Brigitte took James to church every Sunday, that was a given. The whole family was in attendance, as were all good Lutherans. Young James was also in attendance every Wednesday evening from 6:3o – 7:30 for Bible study, as well as Saturday afternoons for prayer meeting. The ladies of the auxiliary prayed for all those in the congregation, the poor children in Africa and the Mormons, all who needed the extra help.

There were also many church functions at which young James was in attendance, there were potlucks, bake sales and the monthly free store when small sundries and foodstuffs were disseminated to the needy. What did James Jr.'s parents think of all this churchy stuff then? They didn't mind in the least. James was a good boy who stayed out of trouble when some youngsters his age were getting into all sorts of crazy things, violent video games, R-rated movies and drinking and whatnot.

There are worse things for a young person than faith. Some of those in the congregation with salacious minds and wagging tongues wondered about such a nice looking young blonde boy (obviously, he took after his father's side) being so often around an apparently celibate priest, but they were just sad old bitches who had nothing better to consume themselves with. No such thoughts had ever occurred to the good and faithful Pastor Jensen. The only person he ever thought about remotely sexually, was Brigitte.

No one ever could have foreseen the tragedy that was to strike our young James.

Now it so happens that many, many years earlier, Pastor Jensen's predecessor, who had been a strong believer in the old ways started an annual Lutefisk traditional supper for the weekend after Easter. That gelatinous looking, horrid smelling, butter drenched traditional Scandinavian specialty that it seems only Americans now consume.

Of course, tradition being what it is this unfortunate supper was continued. Personally, though he would never admit it, Pastor Jensen hated Lutefisk, as do most people. The church basement, which housed the church kitchen and community room fairly stunk like he couldn't even tell what for weeks after. It was all he could do to keep the nauseating smell from invading his own attached home. He was more than happy when Brigitte kindly suggested the Women's Auxiliary take over the planning and execution of the yearly event.

"If you really think you have the time," he replied, all the while thinking to himself, *have at it, and God be with you*, wondering if he could possibly find a reason to be out of town that weekend. Maybe a relative would pass or something.

As the weeks up to Easter approached, and the Women's Auxiliary put the annual Easter egg hunt plans to rest, it was time to start planning for the Lutefisk Supper. Brigitte asked if she might stop by Father Jensen's home Sunday after services to discuss logistics. Important things such as, where are the many pounds of dried cod fish to be purchased, where and how will it be soaked in lye for the week ahead of time?

Wait, you say, *lye*? Yes, that caustic drain cleaner that is used by murderers to dispose of their victims is also used to give Lutefisk its unforgettable texture, smell and taste.

It was only natural that young James came along to the meetings at Father Jensen's home.

During these visits Pastor Jensen and Brigitte would partake of his plentiful stock of Lakka from the bottle kept on the side table in the living room, both being avid drinkers of the stuff. Oddly, during these meetings and perhaps due to the imbibing of the Lakka, Pastor Jensen would wonder what his life may have been like married to this deeply spiritual and good woman before him. But, as we said, if Brigitte ever thought about what might have been, she never gave a conscious indication.

For some reason, these Lutefisk supper meetings were happening with surprising frequency, with young James watching his grandmother and Pastor Jensen the whole time. What Pastor Jensen didn't notice and what Brigitte wouldn't have admitted, she thoroughly enjoyed the old pastor's company. James could tell the subtle differences in his grandmother, both during and afterwards. There were more frequent smiles, the unaware humming of a gay old ditty and the extra care on her appearance. Small things, but they were large in James' mind.

The thought of his grandmother being so happy made James happy. He attributed it to the Lakka though, not Pastor Jensen. He had seen his own parents become quite lively after a couple of drinks and started thinking about what it would be like to have a drink or two.

One such evening, Father Jensen's Lakka bottle was nearly empty and both he and Brigitte had decided they had time for one more small drink.

"James, would you mind running down to the storage room and fetching a bottle?" Pastor Jensen kindly asked.

"No, sir, I wouldn't mind," James replied, always so polite.

"It is up on the high shelf, but there is a tall stool you can use to reach up for it" Pastor Jensen said. "Will you be okay to do it?" He asked James.

"Yes sir," James answered, jumping down from his chair and scurrying down to the basement. Part of the reason James was in such a hurry to fetch the Lakka for Father Jensen was he had overheard some school chums talking about drinking their parent's alcohol and even though at first the taste was awful, and it burned going down, they enjoyed it (they were lying of course, it had made them dizzy and sick).

Now we should mention something Pastor Jensen seems to have forgotten. Several years past, the city council briefly debated about making it illegal to process any food using lye, which basically is a poisonous and dangerous foul liquid. So, fearful of the legal ramifications of their annual Lutefisk dinner and wanting to keep it alive in honor of his predecessor, Pastor Jensen removed all the labels on all the bottles he kept on the high shelf, including the entire case of Lakka he bought that year.

There was absolutely no way James could know which liquid filled bottle was which.

After climbing up on the tall stool to reach the high shelf, James determined that if he took a swig or two out of the bottle neither Pastor Jensen nor his grandmother were likely to notice. Relying on his friend's greater knowledge of such things, the burning sensation and the bad taste of the first swallow convinced James he had found the correct bottle.

He had not.

The End.

KATE

The would-be zombie apocalypse, still being feared by conspiracy theorists everywhere, happened many, many years ago in a small town in Pennsylvania, and was quickly halted by the quick-thinking actions of one young lady, my beloved.

Everyone knows the most feared creatures in our mythology, all of which is true, by the way, have been among us for hundreds, if not thousands of years. Vampyres rose up out of the misguided worship of Selene by some young Greek, pissing Apollo off, and forcing our would-be hero to make a deal with Hades, the god of the underworld. The result was a race of blood sucking night dwellers still residing among us.

Dr. Frankenstein's immortal monster and the many other before and after tests and attempts at perfection, were set free to roam and terrorize in the 1700's. Mark my words, you haven't seen the last of them no matter how many pitchforks you poke them with.

Werewolves, believed to have originated in Wisconsin, can be heard howling during full moons and seen as distant shapes terrorizing sheep farms and hippie communes here and in the UK.

Republicans, er... no, that's another story, Huh? Ha Ha Ha.

But zombies have had their day and are no more, no matter how many TV shows and movies would like you to believe otherwise. What's that? You wonder what exactly were the zombies, and how did they originate? Good questions my fine fellows but my throat is a little too dry to continue.

What? Oh yes, a drink would help immensely.

Simply put, generally a zombie is a mindless flesh-eating animal with no human thoughts or feelings of any kind, reanimated from the dead among us. Zombieism as it is now known, was brought on by a simple cold-like virus transmuted from a certain species of South-American bat, that mutated in humans. It was easily spread by contact with infected saliva. Get bit by a Zombie, die and be a Zombie, very simple, really, huh?

How do I know all this, you ask? I was there. I am Dr. Georgious Pastrolukus, at your service. Most people just call me Dr. George. Why yes, I'd love another drink, thank you.

Now I just happened to be passing through your Pennsylvania on my way to confab with a particularly wise native elder in North Dakota, about the mysterious and sometimes embarrassing profusion of warts on say a, um...particularly embarrassing spot on my anatomy, ahem, when I beheld the most fabulously beautiful young woman I had ever seen.

Her jet-black hair, framing that perfect oval face, with two of the most striking, deep blue eyes.... well, I'd hope there were two, right? Ha Ha Ha. That reminds me of the Cyclops I met on, er..., no never mind about him, he was grumpy most of the time anyway.

Where was I? Oh yes, Elizabeth, with her perfectly round bosoms and her... er, nevermind about that. Poor Elizabeth, what a tragedy.

We gazed at each other, the longing plain in both of our faces, our breath coming in short gasps, like the oxygen had been sucked from the room, her axe striking the porcine carcass just perfectly between the third and fourth... What? Oh, she was the butcher's daughter, what did you think I was talking about? Stop interrupting, will you? There's a good group of fellows. What? Yes, I am ready for another drink, if you don't mind. Thank you.

We were inseparable from that time until Elizabeth's, er..., misfortunes. As I was a little short on disposable funds right at that time as it so happens, Elizabeth persuaded her father to let me stay in the back, upstairs room of the shop in exchange for a little cleaning up and general organizing. My what a system they had, or should I say lack of a system, huh? Ha Ha Ha. I worked my magic, and it was soon running like clockwork. I suspected Elizabeth's father thought I was being over-worked, for I heard him ask her one evening if I just couldn't leave well enough alone, showing how highly he prized my contributions.

It turns out, my sweet, surprising Elizabeth was also an amateur biologist, in her spare time. She had a whole collection of things preserved in jars down in the basement of her Father's shop. Oh, there were hearts, and skulls and eyeballs, rats, bats and pigs feet, er..., wait, no they were mine to snack on. Ha Ha Ha. Do they have any here by chance? What, No? Well, no mind. Well, Elizabeth had just all kinds of God's once living creatures in jars down in that old basement.

"Why, Dearheart," I asked one evening when I happened upon Elizabeth down there tinkering with her collection, "whatever is all this for?"

"I'm studying the biology of living things", she said to me, "in order to help my parents."

"But these specimens are all dead," I intoned, pointing around the room to them.

"They didn't used to be", she answered with a shrug.

Made perfect sense you see, huh?

A thought occurred to me. "Whatever's the matter with the dear Mr. and Mrs. Borden, if I may be so bold as to inquire?" I asked, tentatively setting my hand gingerly on her shoulder, my heartbeat accelerating.

"See that bat over there in that jar?" she asked, pointing with her perfectly shaped finger, to a rather large and gruesome looking creature floating in some kind of brownish liquid. "That's a South American Zombie Bat, and it bit both my parents. My parents are Zombies."

Now as a Doctor, I know a little something about most things, and I know it is purported that the South American Zombie Bat's victims usually die and reanimate, within hours. However, they are extinct. I said all this to my sweet Elizabeth.

"I thought the South American Zombie Bat was extinct?" I questioned.

"They are now", she answered, again pointing to the same jar.

There was only one question left to ask, only one thing to do. "How can I help, my Dear?"

She sighed as delicate sigh as many a stage actress wished she could, with a delicate hand brushing back a lock of ebony hair from her ivory forehead.

"Alas," she said, "all hope is lost. There is only one thing left to do." With a wee tear escaping from under one big beautiful eyelash.

"No!" I gasped.

"Yes, to save all of humanity they must be put down before it is too late." She declared with a look of urgency, sending a chill down my spine.

Ahh, thank you for the handkerchief, my good man. I apologize for my unseemly show of emotion. My poor, brave Elizabeth, I'm not sure I can continue. What, yes, I think another drink would help immensely. Thank you, my fine fellow. Better make it a double though, huh?

"How, how will you, er…, I mean, we… how will we, um make it come about? For your parents, I mean." I asked meekly, not wanting to broach such a delicate subject with my innocent Elizabeth.

With eyes lowered, meekly she said, "What do you think we should do Dr. George?" Her eyelashes batting so prettily, I don't even think she was aware of the effect she had on me, so innocent she was.

I paused for a moment, wanting to gather her up in my arms to console her, but I knew she thought we should wait a seemlier amount of time. After all, we'd only been courting for three months, as she often told me when my passion got the better of me, and I tried to hold her.

"You're pretty darn good with that axe," I said.

"My thoughts exactly," she said scraping her hair back across the old concrete floor, standing and brushing imaginary wrinkles from her dress. She was such a strong, brave woman. My heart swelled with love and pride. "Come on then", she continued, "they are at home on the farm. We can take the carriage."

The carriage ride out to the farm was done in the darkness and silence with Elizabeth leaning up against my arm as I drove, to keep warm in the winter chill. I had many questions about what would happen next. Would we stay in Pennsylvania and marry, or would we go somewhere else to get away from the memories?

Sadly, it wasn't to be.

As we arrived at her parent's farm, Elizabeth noticed they had a guest. "Oh drat, that noisy little neighbor Katherine is here."

"Will that be a problem," I asked.

"Not at all, wait here." She said, as she clutched her axe and climbed down.

I don't like to think about what happened next. My poor Elizabeth having to walk into that farmhouse and save humanity, to save us all from the monsters her parents were sure to become. I longed to go with her, but my sciatica was acting up from the cold, and I didn't think I could get down from the carriage, just then.

I expected gruesome screams, but there was only silence. Then, as if shot out of a gun, a young girl, who I could only assume was the troublesome neighbor, Katherine, fled out the front door, through the snow and into the woods, with poor Elizabeth in hot pursuit, huh? I could only guess, poor little Katherine was also infected. Elizabeth's parents must have turned. We had only just gotten there in the nick of time, but not soon enough to save that poor little girl.

What? No, I think I've had enough, thank you. Yes, yes, I'm nearing the end.

Just as Elizabeth emerged from the woods dabbing something from her face, tears no doubt, I chanced to be looking out across the field to see several carriages of men quickly approaching the farm. Now being no stranger to the dislike and unreasonableness of the local constabulary myself on occasion, I quietly urged the horse onto the opposite lane and away from the farm.

I heard they hung my poor Elizabeth even though I wrote a letter in her defense, unsigned of course, explaining the zombie outbreak. Alas, but to no avail, huh?

Well Sir, I don't exactly know what a 'load of malarkey' is, but I don't think I like your tone.

The End.

LEO

For the artist, the truly creative type who is compelled to follow his or her muse, to these poor souls art becomes like the very air that you or I breath to survive. Without their art, life is nothing but a meaningless, sad and gray world that slowly suffocates the true artist. The creative person, the truly originally creative person is the living, beating heart of the world. Imagine life without Beethoven or Michael Jackson, without Picasso or Sol LeWitt, without Gehry or Frank Lloyd Wright, without Baryshnikov or Martha Graham.

Life would be a series of dull gray days joining end to end.

Yes, we have the Curies and the Hawkins, the Teslas and the Franklins, the Ruths and the Phelps, but these, as great as they are don't bring joy into our lives or hope or wonder. These mirror the intellect and the physical of life, not the heart.

Which would you rather have, a visit to the Guggenheim or Georgia Tech, the Louvre or Lloyds of London, the Hanging Gardens of Babylon, or the Hoover Dam?

When it was announced that there would be a field trip in two weeks to the Wadsworth Atheneum for the whole class, Leo was beside himself with excitement. While most the boys in his class took this news with some mild interest at best, Leo was energized. Leo considered himself a great artist. Leo drew, colored and finger-painted with the best of them. When he compared his masterpiece of, say a Thanksgiving turkey, to those of his classmates, Leo felt only sorrow for his friends who were so obviously bereft of any real talent.

After watching years of Bob Ross' magic oil paintings, Leo couldn't wait until he was old enough for oils so he too could paint like the masters, maybe even as well as Bob Ross himself. Leo gobbled up every PBS show about art and artists he could find, whether it be painting and drawing (his forte), sculpture or basket weaving.

Leo's room and the kitchen refrigerator were practically papered with Leo's drawings and watercolors. Leo was so prolific an artist that he could turn out four or five masterpieces a day, more on the weekends and school breaks. When his father tried to interest him in baseball, Leo used his markers to color that baseball the most interesting psychedelic swirl you've ever seen. When his father tried to unsuccessfully interest Leo in other things boys his age were into, his mother would say "leave him be, he is what he is, it's just a phase." Finally giving up, his father bought Leo the biggest artist's set he could find at Target. It was full of markers, colored pencils, brushes and watercolors galore. Leo loved it. "If you're gonna do it," his Father said, "you need the right tool for the right job."

From his TV shows about artists he always watched, Leo knew the life of the artist could be a tough one for the few weeks it would take to get discovered. Look at Picasso, he had to cut off and sell his ears for money to buy paint. Leo liked his ears and decided he needed a shortcut.

What better place to get discovered than at the art museum. Only the greatest were in Hartford's Atheneum he was sure. That is where his work belonged, he knew without any doubt.

Leo spent the next two weeks feverishly sorting through all his current work in order to select only the best of the best for his upcoming unveiling at the Atheneum. He created new works in a fury of creativity. There was a series of cat watercolors of all sorts because the cat often came into Leo's room while he was creating, and a series of colored pencil sketches of the view outside his bedroom window. He even did a few of his teacher and classmates, all from memory mind you.

Plus, he created new things, alien planet vistas, and wondrous creatures to stir any imagination. He drew scenes from his favorite books and movies. He painted, he drew, he colored. Leo was an artist extraordinaire, his muse in full swing.

The day before the trip to the Atheneum, Leo was trying to decide the best way to affix his works to the museum walls. Now usually he used scotch tape or sometimes even masking tape to place his bedroom art. Out in the kitchen his mother used magnets on the refrigerator. He wasn't sure but he doubted there were any refrigerator doors in the museum to utilize, so magnets probably were out and he was afraid tape wasn't permanent enough, *glue then* he wondered, but he had experience with glue and remembered it could be particularly messy. He didn't want anything messing up his art.

Wandering around the house, he noticed his parent's artwork was hung with nails and wire. That would work fine for things in frames he supposed, but none of his works were yet framed. That doesn't happen until an admirer has purchased them, he was pretty sure. So, nails and wire were out.

He stumbled on his answer more by accident than anything else. That day in class, he noticed on the information board in the classroom that the various things were held in place with tacks. Now tacks had many advantages over his other ideas he thought. They were very permanent things. He knew tacks could be very hard to push in and pull back out, so they probably wouldn't fall out on their own. They were small so he could easily carry as many as he would need and he knew where his mother kept them in the kitchen.

The next morning (the morning of the trip) Leo was up early and dressed in his best suit jacket, bowtie (clip-on), Sunday shoes and all. Once in the kitchen he started rifling through the drawers to get to the tacks. He found them in the left-hand drawer next to the Tic-Tacs.

Finally noticed by his Mother, "What do you need dear," she asked.

"Tacks" he replied, his answer being muffled by the partial pop-tart in his mouth. His mom must have thought he said Tic-Tacs because she told him to bring enough to share with his friends.

At first Leo was perplexed, why would his friends need tacks? Then an uncomfortable thought crossed his mind. What if his friends were also going to use this trip to the museum to display their own works of art? He thought it likely, after all, that's how an artist started. Though he couldn't imagine who of his friends had the talent. Becky Johnson did do a passingly fair Thanksgiving turkey, he supposed.

Now Leo was worried. What if they used up all the best spaces hanging their own work? Leo himself had over forty of his best rolled up and ready to go. There was no way he was sharing his tacks. He saw now that he would need to utilize a stealthier procedure to bring in his art and his tacks into the museum. After much folding and rolling and squeezing and hiding his sandwich in the back of the cabinet, (he kept the Oreos, an artist has to eat after all) he managed to get about 25 pieces into his lunchbox and pockets, plus the tacks. This way too, he would avoid having the museum impound his work if they didn't believe it was his. He didn't want to be accused of stealing from a museum like the old Nazis. (Leo, just maybe, watched too much PBS).

Finally, he and his class arrived at the Atheneum.

The art museum was everything Leo imagined it would be and more! Here was room after room of paintings and other kinds of art in styles and colors and techniques he never dreamed were possible. While many of the children were bored or preoccupied with other thoughts, Leo was enraptured with all the docent was saying. So much so, that he almost forgot his own little supply of masterworks in his New England Patriot's lunchbox (his father had picked it out). Leo pulled on the jacket of his teacher. "I gotta pee," he said. He didn't really have to pee, it was a ruse to get away from the group, a clever one, in Leo's mind.

"Can it wait, Leo?" His teacher asked. I don't know why adults always ask this question, obviously it can't. "Alright, take your trip buddy (everyone had a trip buddy) but hurry right back. The restrooms are in the hallway two rooms back."

"Yes sir," Leo answered. When his teacher turned back to the docent, a particularly attractive and intelligent woman of about the teacher's own age, Leo slipped away without his trip buddy John, whom he didn't really like anyway (he had sweaty hands, and sometimes picked his nose).

Leo chose a room where there was no guard watching. None of the other few adults noticed him. He scooted down behind a round couch in front of one of the largest paintings he had ever seen, and hurriedly opened his lunch box. In fact, he was in such a hurry, as he opened it, the tacks all sprayed out into the room. Guiltily, he scooped up as many as he could, but they had bounced all over the place. He was left with about a handful. Just then, as luck would have it, the guard walked into the room and spying Leo alone, headed over in his direction.

Leo was nearly in full panic mode now. Not only was he carrying a lunchbox full of drawings and paintings he thought they would think he stole, he had just spilled tacks all over the little couch and floor of the room. Desperate to not get in trouble, he placed the lunchbox on the couch and perched on top of it, trying to look innocent and squish it down into the cushions with his little fanny, all at the same time. He had tried to stuff the tacks into his pocket, but they wouldn't go easily.

Any minute the guard was going see all the other tacks, and the ones in Leo's hand and he was going to be in full blown trouble. In Leo's mind there was only one thing to do to avoid getting in to serious trouble. He swallowed all the tacks that he was still holding onto.

The End.

MAUD

The Fluyt was a thing of beauty, riding the waves of the great oceans and seas with a grace and sublimity lacking in other types of trading vessels. Embert stood on the dock outside one of his father-in-law's many warehouses in the port town of Hoorn, marveling at the two- and three-masted ships that lay at anchor waiting to be serviced by the dock workers. Embert loved the slapping of the waves and the taste of salt on the air, the call of seabirds and the yells, songs and curses of the dockside work gangs. The hawking of vendors, the swagger of seamen on leave, the whistles, catcalls and risqué comments for the 'Ladies' as they strolled by displaying their 'wares'. The docks were a lively, busy and occasionally rough place.

The large fleet of Fluyts employed by the majority of the Dutch trading families, including his wife's family, is what has given the Dutch their mastery over the sea-based trade of Scandinavia, Europe, North Africa and India. These 80-foot cargo vessels could be managed by a minimum crew, carried relatively no armaments and therefore were able to be built more cheaply and move faster over the seas. Their speed allowed them to outrun any pirate vessels encountered. Occasionally, the merchant fleet was herded by the larger, older and more powerful galleons or the quicker frigates of the Dutch East India Trading Co's warship fleet.

Traditionally on a trading voyage the cargo master was a member of the family, a son, neer-do-well cousin, son-in-law, etc. The cargo master oversees the coin and the trade, what sells where, what gets purchased etc., while the captain is in charge of the ship itself. To the crew, the cargo master is a respected member of the family, all he had to do for that respect was be born. The Captain was a seaman who earned his respect through hard work and experience. Little rivalry exists between the two, for both know they must work together to make a successful voyage. For one to override the other's decision, there had better be compelling reason.

In just a fortnight, Embert was to make his first trading voyage as cargo master, on a lone trading vessel, the Beverielle. Embert felt honored to be appointed such by his father-in-law, even if it was just the one ship. The Beverielle was to depart Hoorn for Christiana with a supply of expensive rare spices and perfumes to be sold to the highest bidders among the factors there. After unloading, the Beverielle's next custom was at the discretion of the cargo master. He may play it safe and pick up furs and lumber at a set price or, if he makes good contacts, may hear of a better trade elsewhere. Under no circumstances would the ship return empty. There may be three or four additional trade stops before returning to Hoorn with whatever cargo the cargo master decided upon, and with whatever coin garnered in his trades. The Beverielle may be out for three weeks or three months. With Embert chomping to prove himself to his father-in-law and new wife, anything might possibly happen.

On the Hoorn to Christiana route, there was little chance of pirates unless they be pirates off the English isle, so there was no escort planned. The German ocean could be treacherous with large ice floes and floating bergs that could be unpredictable. Pirates tended to the warmer southern seas of the Atlantic and Mediterranean. However on this occasion, while Embert was pouring over charts and logs and trading accounts and preparing for his voyage, on the north-western coast of Scotland, what may have been the world's unluckiest pirate was himself preparing for a journey.

Ferguson Aberdeen, aka Ferg the Fearless, "inherited" his ship from its previous owner in a card game, after the previous owner's untimely demise. You might think winning a pirate ship in a card game takes some luck, but you've never seen the Black Death. The Black Death was the most rat-infested, barnacle encrusted, leaky death trap to ever put to sea. Its keel was warped, its bow crooked, its steering wheel off center, its rudder was cracked and the sails were the worst, moth eaten, moldy and holey things to ever be run up a mast. The Black Death has killed many a sailor but unfortunately, mostly her own. The traditional pirate flag itself was so faded and torn that most people thought it was just an off-white smudge on a graying background. We shouldn't even mention what the crew was like. About all of them being one-eyed, peg-legged, pock-faced broken-down murderers, rapists and thieves. Oh, and one Lutheran.

"You sail in that thing?" It was often asked, 'You must be fearless," (i.e. completely cracked), thus 'Ferg the Fearless'.

Now the Black Death wasn't the only part of Ferg's life that indicated some passing familiarity with bad luck. Ferg's homely wife, Mathilda, died giving birth to Ferg's only would-be son, taking the poor little tyke with her to hell or wherever. Ferg was left with one child, a daughter, Maud. Maud was too young to be left alone and as everyone knows, it was extremely unlucky to have a female of any age aboard a ship. Ferg decided to pass Maud off as a boy. With her short-shorn hair, grime-covered exterior and non-descript clothes, no one could tell the difference anyway.

As a pirate, plying the waters of the German ocean was as good a plan as any, there being little competition and little expectation by merchant ship captains of pirates. Assuming you could avoid the freezing fogs, floating castles of ice, treacherous currents and colder-than-balls temperatures. In a fast ship the German ocean could be sailed in each direction in as little as a few days. Quick out and strike, quick back in to count your plunder was the plan, if your luck was with you.

The Black Death was put to rights, as much as was possible. Provisions were stowed, water barreled, powder and shot made ready. As he and his crew worked, Ferg never dreamed what a prize he was going to encounter in the Beverielle.

The Black Death's second mate was a particularly unlikeable, greasy, bad-tempered, lout who liked to fight, drink, gamble and screw, pretty much in that order. He had come with the ship. The crew knew and if not liked, at least respected his ability with his fists and his knowledge of curse words.

On the morning of the day the Black Death was going to set sail, the Quarter Master (the man in charge of ship and crew), a barely more respectable man than the first mate was killed in a back-alley knife fight.

As soon as the news was relayed to the Black Death, a melee of astronomical proportions broke out among the crew. After all, it is how promotions are decided on a Pirate ship. Last man standing, and all that. The former second mate survived to become the Quarter Master and so on down the line, positions were re-ordered. Cuts and gashes were sewed, blood sopped up, mead and congratulations passed around.

When Ferg boarded the Death with a youngster in tow, if the crew had any thoughts about it, they kept them to themselves. What business of theirs was it? A nephew, wanting to be a sailor, they had heard it said. He kept to himself, and no more thought was accorded him.

"Raise the anchors and make sail toward Christiana" Ferg ordered the sailing master.

Now just about anyone could own a ship, but he important thing was the charts one owned. The charts were the most securely guarded treasure of a ship's captain. Without the charts, no one would know how to get where they wanted to be. So, a few more directions were required, "steer Nor Nor'West at 18 degrees," type of thing. You see, the thing about sailing a ship was you don't really have to detour for much. You could pretty much go in a straight line if you knew how, otherwise you just went in circles.

Off went the Black Death, zig-zagging across the German Ocean toward Christiana. A look out had to be kept the whole way for the tell-tale signs of a sail on the horizon, which would indicate their prey. After about two weeks of sailing, avoiding icebergs and whatever sea monsters lurked thereabouts, the Death still hadn't spotted any other ships.

"Should we go closer to land, Cap'n?" the new Quarter Master asked, anxious to do some plundering and what not, during one of the brief times they were both on the poop deck. "Not much out 'ere but bergs 'n cold."

Ferg considered. If they moved in closer to the Denmark coast, they would probably have more luck, but there may be patrols out as well. It has been two weeks and the crew were starting to grumble. Ferg knew it was not uncommon for a pirate ships crew to remove the captain for any number of reasons, no booty being chief among them.

"Is that your recommendation then?" Ferg asked, more to be able to share the blame if something went wrong than for any other reason. "Closer on to Denmark then," Ferg directed the Sailing Master, who was listening intently to the exchange between the Quarter Master and Captain, in case things went badly.

Almost immediately, down from the crow's nest came the words "sail ho", indicating a ship had been spotted on the horizon, making it between two and three miles away. Immediately all three men snapped open their 'Netherlands Telescopes' the single, hand-held spyglass just recently invented.

"Dutch India Trading," muttered the Quarter master, spying the flags.

"Looks as though it is headed straight for us," Ferg replied. "I don't see any others."

"A fat prize, then," the greasy quartermaster exclaimed.

"Raise the Dutch flag," the captain yelled, the order being repeated down the length of the deck. The crew ran to do their captain's bidding from among the many flags available. "Make your heading 5 degrees starboard," He told the Sailing Master, "You there," pointing to the chief, "spill the wind."

"Cap'n," inquired the Quarter Master? Even though the Quarter Master was basically in charge of ship and crew, it was the Captain who plotted the course, devised strategy and ruled absolutely during all engagements.

"If we come straight at them they will turn with the wind and flee, and we will not be able to catch them, that Fluyt is too fast for us. If we turn now and slow, we can turn into them at the last moment, come up alongside and board them with ease, maybe hit them with a broadside." The captain explained to respectful and hopeful faces all around, fighting and not strategy being the crews' strong point. After all, this is why they have a captain.

"Ready the port guns but keep the ports closed," the captain yelled and again his orders were repeated down into the ship as men ran to their posts. Fortunately for Ferg, the wind was behind them, meaning the Beverielle was having to tack into the wind. Timed just right as they tacked to their starboard, Ferg could order his ship to port, and close the distance twice as fast, catching them unawares.

Over on the Beverielle they had also spotted the Black Death, and not recognizing it was suspiciously watching it to see what its captain and crew would do.

"They are turning to their starboard, Sir," yelled the lookout, to the relief of many. "Dutch colors flying."

"Beat to quarters," the captain of the Beverille demanded and drum beats tolled out, calling all crewmen to stations, and all officers to the bridge. He was not one to take chances. When he could see the Dutch uniforms, then he would relax. When Embert made it to the bridge and was apprised of the situation he felt there was nothing to worry about. Another Dutch ship would never attack them so he asked for his leave to return to his cabin, where he had been counting coins and notating registers.

He was below minutes later when the ship shuddered and groaned mightily like a gigantic hand had slapped it. He and all his coin tossed about the tiny cabin like flotsam, and then all hell broke out.

At the last possible second, just as the Beverielle was starting its starboard tack, Ferg ordered all sails full and ordered the turn into the oncoming ship. "Roll out the guns!" Ferg yelled, and the men below strained to do it, getting ready to fire the first volley, as they turned back for the broadside. "Prepare to board!" he ordered the rest of the waiting crew. The Quarter Master could already taste sweet victory. *This captain knew his stuff!* He thought with greed in his heart.

It was a nicely executed plan, or it would have been except for Ferg's traditionally bad luck. Just as both ships were headed almost straight at each other, the Black Death's rudder snapped completely in half. With sails on full and the wheel spinning out of control, impact was inevitable, even though the Beverielle tried to turn with all her might, with her bells clanging ferociously.

Ferg's ship smashed into the Beverielle just forward of midstern, and broke apart with crew, cargo and ship's parts being flung into the ice-cold sea. The poor old Black Death had taken too much strain over her long years of pirating and icy cold death poured into her belowdecks. The Beverielle, though heavily damaged managed to stay afloat.

Some few of the Death's crew were rescued, including the Quarter Master, just to be unceremoniously hanged for piracy. Many more met again in Davey Jones's locker. Maud, who had been laying on her small cot in the captain's cabin due to having caught a sickness some days before, wearing the type of sleeping gown all children of the age wore, floated away on a broken piece of galley table, too small to be seen by the busy crew of the Beverielle.

Neither Ferg nor Maud was ever seen again. As for the Beverielle, it limped into a nearby Danish port, having made a tidy profit on its original cargo. The sailors of the Beverielle drank for many a night on tales of the vicious pirate attack and ramming they had survived, by the grace of Neptune himself.

The End.

NEVILLE

Part 1.

Few things generate the kind of warmth in a man's heart than does the feeling he gets when he returns home to a happy and loving family after a hard day's work. Bob Cratchitt, from that other story, certainly felt that way as did our John Farrow, the fellow whose family this story is about.

Now by almost anyone's account John Farrow was a lucky man. He had been born handsome and sturdy of mind and body into a well-off family, being educated at some of England's best institutions. He met and married the beautiful, smart and engaging Claudette. They had two of the most wonderful, happy and well-mannered children a man could hope for, Louise and Neville, children who were a pleasure to speak with and spend time with. John's children were inquisitive, kind, intelligent and energetic.

Louise and Neville engaged with their tutors on a much higher level than the ordinary children their ages. They were interested in history, science, mathematics, art and music. Louise could dance and played two instruments, the flute and violin. In addition to enjoying sculpture, and being a passingly fine alto, Neville was athletic, excelling in football and cricket, and also had a deft hand at the violin.

There wasn't a moment in their home that the conversations weren't lively, engaging and even sometimes funny. Never was a cross word spoken, or an exasperated look passed. At supper, which may have been prepared by any one, or all of them, conversations were sometimes serious, sometimes light-hearted but always filled with wonder, the love and respect shared among them apparent to any onlookers, who may have been fortunate enough to have been invited into their home.

Yes, John Farrow was a lucky man indeed, until the day the tragedy struck.

It started out like any other of a hundred Sundays for the Farrow family. As was their habit, Church was skipped, the Farrows being scientifically inclined, had gravitated more toward a humanist view, rather than religious. The warm and breezy day called for tea and croissants on the back patio, while the paper was digested, the politics debated, and the arts scene section exclaimed over.

"Oh look, this lecture at the Natural History museum on Wednesday evening looks positively enthralling," exclaimed Louise. Then they all laughed at Neville's mock look of disdain, for all present knew he loved the Natural History museum.

"We'd love to go honey," Mrs. Farrow said, "But Judith and Lee are coming over to play pinochle," to John's mock look of disdain (they all knew John loved to play pinochle) and after chuckling, she continued, "It is our turn to host, after all."

"Well, next time then," Louise said a little disappointedly.

"Hey," Neville said, to try to shore up Louise's spirits, "You and I could go to the library instead that night and see if they have Theodore Dreiser's new book yet. I heard it was great!"

"Oh yes," Louise replied, brightening immensely. "If it's Okay with you Mummy and Daddy?"

"That sounds perfect," John Farrow said, "but don't you two be going in there and causing a ruckus," he finished while jokingly wagging a finger at his two perfectly behaved children.

Everyone laughed.

Later that afternoon they were all dead, except for Neville, who had gotten not even a scratch from the horrific accident that killed the rest of his family.

Now John and Claudette Farrow had been only children, having no siblings. Both sets of their parents had also previously passed, John's on a missionary trip to Africa where apparently they had been mistaken for dinner and Claudette's on the ill-fated maiden voyage of the Titanic. You might think that left poor Neville in the care of the state but it just so happened John Farrow had a spinster aunt. A mean, over-weight, unkempt, penny-pinching ornery old biddy with a big wart on the end of her nose, with hairs growing out of it.

This was the woman whom they saw once a year for three hours every Christmas Eve, and who acted so put upon to have to host them for that long. It was three hours of noxious smells (from the surrounding moors everyone hoped), noisome complaints about the state of life in general and the yappy little dog she kept for company. The poor dog never seemed to leave her lap, being fed a constant stream of disgusting looking tidbits from a plate on the side table. If she had ever given the children even some token Christmas gift, a pat on the head or said a kind word, they would have been sure it was an imposter in her place.

This is the woman Neville now had to live with, for strangely John and Claudette had failed him miserably in that they had left no will and no designated guardian. It was a gaping hole in their otherwise perfectly lived and planned lives, and the devoted care of their children.

Part 2.

At first Neville hardly noticed (or smelled) his surroundings. He slept. He woke and got up. If there was food down in the kitchen, he ate. He kept completely to himself in the beginning and stayed mostly in his room high up in the castle-type house Aunt Clerdance kept as her home. He didn't read, he didn't converse, he didn't do much of anything but mourn. Aunt Clerdance didn't intrude, you might think out of respect for his grief, but that would take some human feeling of which Aunt Clerdance had none. She just didn't care.

Children however are resilient. And Neville was taught a certain outlook on life that tended toward optimism. Eventually a feeling that a life well lived would be the best tribute to his parents and sister he could create started to take hold. One morning, after hearing kitchen noises, he went down to engage Aunt Clerdance in some plan for his future, and perhaps get to know the woman who was now his only living relative.

"Oh, it lives," was all she said from the side table where she sat with the ever-present dog, as he entered the old, drafty kitchen. "I thought gremlins were stealing my food all this time." For the first time in his short life, Neville was unsure of how to respond, never before having encountered personal disdain.

"Listen boy, watch yourself around here, if you think that paltry monthly pittance your lawyers graciously allow me is enough to feed and clothe you and get you tutors and all, you're sadly mistaken. 3000 pounds isn't what it used to be. This isn't your parent's house, you know." She berated without even looking at him, more interested in her toast and jam. "And I don't want to be hearing any noise. My Fifi doesn't like noise, and I get sick headaches real bad, so I don't want to hear any noise either, understand? And I saw that violin case you brought in, don't even think about it," She paused to take a breath and Neville mistakenly thought her tirade was at an end.

"And don't be going out onto the moors, they are treacherous. About the only thing they are good for is to keep visitors away. I don't need to have to be paying someone to go find your body out there. Best if you just stay upstairs in your room. I saw you brought some books so don't be bothering with my library, either," She finally finished, obviously dismissing him once again from her mind.

Neville was getting to know quite strongly that this was indeed, not his parent's warm, loving home.

"And make sure you clean up after yourself, I'm not your maid," She added with a sniff.

Neville turned and fairly ran up to his room. If Aunt Clerdance noticed, she gave no outward sign as she slurped down her morning tea and gave Fifi the last of her toast and jam.

Nothing his parents taught him prepared him for this new, empty life. With no love, no support but the mean basics, no stimulating discussions, no art or music, no new books, Neville fell into a fugue of staring out his window for most of the day into the cold, desolate moor. When even that became too much trouble, Neville's mind fled, and then he 'shrugged off this mortal coil' completely.

Aunt Clerdance didn't even notice until the smell that wafted from upstairs became the over-powering stench in the old house.

The End.

OLIVE

There once was a story told about a poor shoemaker, his kind wife and some industrious dwarves who helped out with the work. You may have even heard the story yourself, for as all great and true stories, it has spread the world round. Yes, the story of the dwarves and the shoemaker is a true story, but most of the facts have become a little skewed over time.

Foremost, in the story the dwarves were nice little industrious things who helped the shoemaker because he and his wife were good people who helped others. A nice thought, unfortunately it is also very, very wrong.

The dwarves were evil, flea-ridden, rotten little miscreants.

Secondly, the version of the story you are familiar with mentions nothing of the shoemaker and his wife's daughter, Olive. In the real version you are about to read, Olive was very much a part of this story. In fact, without Olive, there'd be no story.

It actually happened thus:

Once upon a time there was a shoemaker who worked very hard at trying to cheat his customers by producing cheap, ill-fitting, grossly-overpriced shoes out of rotted leather he bought at a discount. Still he could not earn enough to live upon and at last all he had in the world was gone, save just leather enough to make one last pair of crappy shoes.

"You are a terrible provider," Mrs. Shoemaker said.

"You are also a terrible father," Olive Shoemaker added.

"You are a terrible wife and child," Mr. Shoemaker replied.

This type of conversation went on all day, every day in the Shoemaker home, largely ignored by all involved until it was their turn to reply.

"You are a lousy shoemaker," Mrs. Shoemaker said.

"You are a lousy father," Olive Shoemaker added.

"You are a lousy wife and child," Mr. Shoemaker replied.

Now as it happens, Mr. Shoemaker's plan was to produce one more pair of crappy, over-priced shoes, in the hopes of selling them for enough to some unsuspecting passer-by, in order to leave the little village on the edge of the magical wood, and his family forever. (Apparently, shoes were very hard to come by and were very, very valuable.)

Then he cut his leather out, all ready to make up the next day, meaning to rise early in the morning to his work. His conscience was clear and his heart light amidst all his troubles, like all truly bad men.

That night, long after Mr. and Mrs. Shoemaker finally stopped sniping and fell asleep, and both started horribly snoring and passing gas Olive Shoemaker hurriedly dressed in her gingham dress with the white around the collar and sleeves (her only dress), put her hair into one long braid and slipped out the window of her corner of the shack. Off she ran into the magical wood, that which the village sits next to, as she did most nights.

Olive had heard from a troll, who had heard from a gypsy, who had the story straight from the baker's boy that a little band of dwarves was seen camping in the forest. Now Olive knew from having heard many years ago that dwarves were magical and that if one was fortunate enough to guess a dwarf's name, that dwarf was forever in your power.

Olive had a plan. An evil, nasty plan, befitting evil, nasty dwarves. Olive would find the Dwarves campsite, sneak up close and hide, all the while listening intently to their conversation in hopes of learning one or the other's name, which she would then use to enslave the dwarves and make them do her will. A good plan, all in all, if you happen to be a nasty, evil git like our Olive.

Surprisingly, the dwarf campsite wasn't that difficult to find (just follow the smell). But when Olive gingerly approached, she noticed another person had already snuck up and was crouched in the bushes listening to the dwarves' conversation. The two ugly little green dwarves were sitting near a fire, sucking on some bones. Assuming this other person was there for the same reason, Olive snuck up behind him and hit him in the head with a rock, knocking him out cold. When Olive turned the boy over, she realized it was the self-same baker's boy. Olive felt a momentary pang of regret, not because she clonked him on the head, but because she didn't really have the time to do certain things to him while he was unconscious.

After a while of scratching and listening, Olive's efforts were finally rewarded when one of the dwarf's used the other dwarf's name.

"You are smelling particularly ripe this evening, my dear friend," said the first dwarf to the other.

"Ahh, thank you kind brother" the other dwarf replied, after lifting an arm to take a sniff.

"Actually, I was referring to your rank breath," replied the first dwarf.

"Must be that small child I consumed earlier," said the other, "it needed changing."

"But you did change it, into a meal!" The first dwarf exclaimed, laughing gaily and slapping his knee at his own small wit.

The other dwarf also found this uproarious and laughing heartily said, "Mumblebuttkerson, you slay me!"

While the dwarves in question were busy laughing and back slapping, Olive sprung up with her braid a-swinging with an "Ah-Ha!" and yelled out, pointing, "Mumblebuttkerson, I compel you!" Thinking all the while that this sounded like the correct wording for a very official compelling.

The dwarves' laughter stopped immediately, for it was no small thing to compel a dwarf.

"Why you nasty little..." started the dwarf known as Mumblebuttkerson, jumping up with hands on hips, obviously quite angry.

"Whatcha gonna make him do for you?" the other dwarf asked Olive, unsuccessfully trying to keep a smirk off his face, lounging back on his elbows.

"You mean, what am I going to make you both do?" Olive replied triumphantly.

"You don't compel me, Olive (dwarves know things, like people's names). I didn't hear my name cross your gnarly lips," replied the first dwarf with a look of satisfaction on his ugly little green face, wagging a finger in her direction.

"His name is Mumblekuttberson," said Mumblebuttkerson, starting a row between the dwarves that lasted well into fifteen minutes before Olive thought to yell "Mumblekuttberson and Mumblebuttkerson, stop!"

Immediately the dwarves ceased all things.

"May we at least breathe?" one of them gasped.

"What, yes of course. Keep breathing," Olive commanded, and the dwarves resumed breathing. As Olive will learn it is a terrible power this compulsion of dwarves. One must be very careful with the wording for dwarves are tricky and if you leave your command open to even the smallest interpretation, it will be your undoing. The dwarves had already tricked Olive into commanding them to stay alive, for no subsequent compulsion can undo a previous one, that's something they don't tell you in dwarf compulsion 101 or wherever.

Now that they weren't fearing for their lives, they settled down a bit. Poor Olive hadn't much imagination or she could have accomplished great things with two magical dwarves at her beck and call. Her only plan was the same as her father's drab, unimaginative plan, except she would be the one to sell the shoes and move far, far away.

Olive told the dwarves what they were to do.

In the morning after Mr. Shoemaker had completed his bathroom chores,

"Open the window!" Mrs. Shoemaker yelled from the bedroom,

he sat himself down to his work; when, to his great wonder, there stood the shoes already made, upon the table. Mr. Shoemaker, for a wonder, knew not what to say or think at such an odd thing happening. He looked at the workmanship; there was not one false stitch in the whole job; all was so neat and true, that the shoes were quite a masterpiece, even the rotted old leather looked new.

The dwarves had done exactly as Olive had commanded and created a beautiful pair of valuable footwear, then disappeared into the wood to stay quietly hidden until Olive's next chore for them. Before Olive could snatch up the shoes and run away with them, a customer came in and the shoes suited him so well that he willingly paid a price higher than usual for them; and the poor shoemaker, with the money and grandiose thoughts of fabulous wealth, bought leather enough to make two pairs more.

Olive was pissed, but upon thinking about it decided two pair were better than one so that night after Mr. Shoemaker cut out the work and went to bed early, she again traveled into the wood and compelled the dwarves to do the same, but twice this time. The only difference being the dwarves were commanded to stay in the attic all the next day in case she needed them, unless directed otherwise.

When he got up in the morning the work was done ready to his hand. Immediately, before Olive could rise (she was a bit lazy in the mornings) in came buyers, who paid him handsomely for the shoes, and out Mr. and Mrs. Shoemaker went, to do some shopping and dining, and to purchase more leather.

"Well, hell," thought Olive. "This ain't happening again," she declared. After dressing in her best (and only) dress and putting her hair into its signature braid, up to the attic she went.

"Listen, Mumbles (she had earlier compelled them to shorten their names for convenience), tonight when that old fool and his smelly old wife return with the new leather, I want you to first take this awl and stab through the eyeballs anyone through the front door. Then make as many beautiful pair of shoes there is leather for and leave them on the table."

"Of course," said one.

"Our pleasure," said the other, with a little bow.

Confident in her plan, Olive prepared to go into town on what she hoped was her last night to have her way with the baker's boy. Before she was quite able to leave though, Mr. and Mrs. Shoemaker were returning down the lane. These circumstances were about to satisfy the letter of the law, as it were, in the dwarves' mind. They prepared to stick their awl through the eyeballs of whomever was through the door first, be it Mr. or Mrs.

Now it is well known, the only way a dwarf can be freed from the compulsion of one who called out his name was with that person's death, the more violent the better, cancelling all previous (and obviously) any future compulsions. So a dwarf will analyze each and every command carefully to see if he can use it to bring about the demise of the compulsor, as it were.

As Mr. and Mrs. Shoemaker approached the front yard, Olive opened the door and quickly ran out, hoping to avoid her nasty parents. Just then a large awl came hurtling through the air from the attic window, piercing Olive through both eyeballs. Immediately after, two green, smelly, ugly dwarves jumped down from the attic window and laughed and capered all the way down the lane.

Upon seeing this turn of events and gazing at poor Olive's body, Mrs. Shoemaker said, "You are a terrible father, Mr. Shoemaker."

"And you are a terrible mother," replied Mr. Shoemaker.

And into the house they went.

The End.

PRUE

Back in the day, when trains were the preferred long-distance mode of transport, Kansas City was the gateway to the west. A busy mish mash of everything that makes the United States such a great and interesting place. And like all American cities, large and small, the 1970's saw its steady decline into inner-city poverty rife with racial tensions, street corners strewn about with refuse and despondent persons of little means.

One thing Kansas City never lost though, was the cowboy. Whether it was due to the agricultural exchanges and livestock auction houses, which were an ongoing concern, or just because some people can never give up the past. It was a common sight to see cowboys strolling down the streets of Kansas City or driving around town in their Ford pick-up trucks and shiny Eldorados, depending on their individual states of prosperity.

Another common sight in Kansas City were the saloons. Real cowboy bars that served whiskey, Anheuser on draft and the occasional pound and a half of sirloin, charred on the outside, red on the in. This is where men would join one another after a hard day's work at the factory, at the livestock houses, or at some downtown office. What you did for a living didn't matter if you were sporting the hat, the boots and the attitude. Now these weren't the types of places where you brought the little miss on a Saturday eve for line dancing. No, these were real bars for real men, Republicans mostly, places where 'Political Correctness' would never get a foot in the door, where men drank, spit and told tall tales, and where the TV was tuned to channel nine to watch Larry Moore every night for the six-o'clock news. If there was a woman present, the term "Lady" had to be applied loosely.

Now it just so happened that a terrible heat wave gripped Kansas City and much of the midwest for 17 days in July 1980. Each one of those terrible days the mercury climbed above 100, and each one of those terrible days, old people died and tempers frayed.

It wasn't the most fortuitous time to visit, but that is just what Frank, Gladys and their daughter Prue were doing, having stopped at the downtown Hyatt Regency for a few nights to visit the Worlds of Fun theme park, for a family vacation. (Yes, the same Hyatt Regency where just the following year terrible tragedy would strike.)

They had been planning their family vacation for some time. Once school finally ended and as the days grew longer, Prue's patience with the wait grew shorter.

"Mom! How many days till we leave now," she would demand to be told daily since the trip was announced.

"Eight, dear," her mother replied, or six or four or whatever the case happened to be.

Until one day, "tomorrow, dear," was the answer. Prue whooped and hollered and ran through the house scaring the poor cat half to death and fluttering the World of Fun brochure behind her like a banner.

Early the next morning, with her father out in the driveway stowing luggage in the way back of the big Pontiac wagon, and her mother giving the neighbor boy last minute directions on caring for the cat and watering the house plants, Prue was surreptitiously trying to stow her favorite doll Gertrude, into her little backpack, even though her mother told her Gertrude couldn't come. Gertrude would go with them, Prue thought. She couldn't leave Gertrude alone for so long and she doubted the older boy from next door would look after her and sing to her and give her tea, like Prue did. Her mother need not know.

Finally, Prue successfully stuffed Gertrude down into the bottom of the little backpack only having to remove the yucky absorbent underpants her mother sometimes made her wear to make enough room and hid them under her mattress. Only little, little kids wear those Prue thought, and Prue vowed to be extra careful.

Soon they were all loaded into the car and on the way.

The trip to Kansas City was uneventful. They stopped along the highway to eat and to pee. They played the license plate game. Prue colored some, though if she did it for too long in the car, she felt icky.

They spent the first night in some motel, which didn't sit well with Prue.

"Are we there? Is this it? I don't see it! You said we'd be there today," Prue accused with a quivering bottom lip, as they unloaded the car in the parking lot, clutching her little pack loath to let it out of her sight.

"Honey, I said we'd leave today, which we did. We will be there tomorrow." Her mother replied, giving her a quick hug and a little push toward the room.
"Ugh," Prue replied, feeling annoyed and a little disappointed, but she brightened when she remembered she had Gertrude in the bottom of her backpack.

They ate the dinner her father had gone out and got while sitting on the bed in front of the TV. Then a moment of truth came.

"Prue honey, do you think you should wear your special underpants to bed? We don't want to mess up the nice cot they brought for you," her mother asked. "Here go get your pack for me and I will get them out."

"Um," was all Prue could think to say, standing half in and half out of the little bathroom with one thumb in her mouth.

"Take your thumb out of your mouth dear," her mother said. "You're too old for that."

"I'm too old for those baby underwears," Prue answered, suddenly feeling inspired.

"Well, if you think so," her mother said with only a little doubt in her voice.

After having an early breakfast in the motel lobby with some of the other overnight guests, to each and every one of whom Prue told she was on her way to World of Fun, their reactions entirely dependent on whether or not they succeeded in having their first cup of coffee, the little family resumed their trip.

"How long now?" Prue asked, fearing the answer, for she was anxious to get there.

"We will be there by lunchtime dear," her mother said to Prue's renewed whoops.

The big Pontiac wagon pulled into the World of Fun parking lot just a little before noon, navigating to a spot among all the other wagons and family sedans that seemed to fill the lot in every direction.

The first day at World of Fun was wonderful to Prue. There were fun musical shows, rides that were fast or scary or high up, characters all dressed up roaming the park, and there was soda and balloons and funnel cakes. There was even (shudder) a haunted house! It was everything Prue hoped it would be. Plus, best of all, Prue gets to come back tomorrow and do even more!

Later that day when they pulled in front of the big hotel in downtown Kansas City, Prue was still busy looking at the World of Fun park map, making her plans for tomorrow's adventure. Her mind so occupied, she totally left her pack and Gertrude in the back seat of the wagon. After her parents commented on the unusual and unexpected heat to seemingly everyone they encountered and made their plans to go down to the restaurant for dinner, they went up and settled into their room.

Now well after supper, when everyone was in bed and asleep, Prue woke, remembering she had left poor Gertrude down in the car in the bottom of that stuffy pack. Knowing Gertrude must be scared (Prue would be), she was determined to go down and rescue her. After all, she knows what the car looks like and it was parked right in front of the big doors. (Prue knew nothing of valet parking.)

As quiet as a mouse she slipped on her flip-flops, could just reach up to undo the door chain and slipped quietly out of the room into the bright, quiet hallway. She had no room keys, no car keys, no identification; just a small girl in her night dress and short robe and flip-flops.

Finding the elevators gave Prue a small challenge but eventually she came across them, punched the button with the arrow pointing down and patiently waited until the whirring stopped and the doors slid open. Stepping in, she was momentarily flummoxed as to which button to push and guessing between the M, L, B1 and B2, selected the correct one.

The doors opened into a deserted lobby, the night manager being in the back office doing the night audit. Prue could see the front doors from the elevator, so she scurried across the carpeted lobby, past the fountain and front desk and out and into the night. It was very warm outside, still being in the mid 90s with very high humidity. As Prue scampered down the steps to find Gertrude and the car, she realized two things, the car was nowhere to be seen, and she really, really had to pee.

Now about this time, the game between the Kansas City Royals and their arch-nemesis the Minnesota Twins was just ending after going 12 innings. The argument in the nearby Steers Head Saloon and Bar (and many other bars around town, I'm sure) was about a questionable 'out' call by the home plate umpire on an attempted steal by the Royals causing Kansas City to lose. Between the unbearable heat and humidity of the last few days, the unfair and prejudicial game call and the flowing Anheuser on tap, tempers were exploding and punches were about to be thrown.

Prue would have turned around to go back into the hotel lobby, if not just at that moment, the nighttime doorman returned from his own call of nature, taking his station outside the hotel door once again. Becoming desperate to pee, and not wanting to reveal her lack of control to her mother who would insist Prue put on the special undies, Prue ran around the corner in search of a restroom and maybe be lucky enough to find the car. Spying what appeared to be an open restaurant across the street (restaurants always had restrooms), Prue carefully looked for traffic both ways and ran across and reached up to open the door.

In the Steers Head Saloon and Bar, which Prue had mistaken for a restaurant, not only were punches thrown, but a full-fledged brawl was currently ongoing and was even then preparing to roll out onto the sidewalk.

Prue was just one of many victims to the heat wave that summer in Kansas City, though her demise was significantly more painful than most. Gertrude hadn't suffered at all.

The End.

QUENTIN

As unusual as it may sound, young Quentin spent his whole life in and around mires. Quentin's father is geography chair at Cambridge University in England and has been the world's foremost researcher into the effect bog lands and mires have on global warming (quite a bit, it seems). Some of the world's largest mires are in Russia and what is now Estonia. Matsalu National Park in Estonia with its huge mires is the most important stopover and feeding site for migratory birds on their journey between the Arctic and western Europe. Vast amounts of peat are exported from Estonia, harvested from the mires, where the peat layer can be as deep as 17 meters.

Mires also have a dark and mysterious history, especially in Estonian folklore. Stand out on the mire some early morning as the spectral mist slowly rises, and the keening of the eastern winds call out to you, you will see why. Many a person has been lost in the mires, seemingly solid ground giving way unexpectedly to a foul, watery death. Do these unfortunate souls rise again each morning, calling out to others to join them or to release them? Some believe so and it is said you will be ensorcelled by them into going out into the mire if you are not on your guard.

Quentin and his Father believed none of these things. They were after all, scientists. At least Quentin's father was, and he taught Quentin to look at all things with an analytical mindset, not a superstitious one.

At first when accompanying his father on summer research trips, Quentin didn't like the bog lands. He thought they smelled awful (it's the methane) and were ugly places. What Quentin did like to do was to collect butterflies. We've all seen a butterfly collection, the poor beautiful creatures staked out onto a board and displayed behind glass like some sort of evil scientist was practicing torture techniques on the tiny, helpless things.

English boys like Quentin particularly like to collect butterflies and display them so. I blame the weather, and the food.

Once Quentin realized the mires were a bountiful buffet of insects, including butterflies, he began to look forward to his summer trips with his father and his father's research team. He began to build a particularly grand and grotesque collection of splayed butterflies, the envy of all his little equally sadistic classmates. After catching the harmless creatures, Quentin used to suffocate the butterflies in a jar, but that took several days before he could add them to his collection. Instead he started piercing their little heads with pins, to speed along the process. This being marginally better than pinning them to his boards alive and waiting for them to die *en place* with their little wings weakly fluttering. His mother forbade him to do that.

When Quentin learned that his father's team was planning a trip to the Matsalu National Park in Estonia, he knew he had to go. The mires in Estonia being one of the only places in the world Quentin could now hope to find the Clouded Apollo butterfly, which he desperately wanted to add to his collection, since a classmate at school had done so. (His had been sent by an uncle, but Quentin vowed to only include butterflies in his own collection he personally tracked and caught.)

Plans were made, grants were filed, visas acquired. The trip would be for twelve days for Quentin, his father and the three members of the research team. Sad that not one soul among them would make it back alive, but mires can be unforgiving places.

Quentin was as good as anyone in safely traversing a mire. He was able to spot the minute color variations that foretold either a patch of thick, safe peat, or just a thin layer that would give way as soon as a foot touched down. His father didn't worry about Quentin coming to harm and succumbing to a watery death.

Quentin's father, his team and Quentin arrived at the edge of the Matsalu National Park in United Nations provided Land Rovers. But that is as far as they could go in the Rovers for from there they must backpack into the Park and onto the mire, where they would set up their camp and equipment. Their UN drivers helped them unload.

Just as the team was getting ready to hike in, resembling so many two-legged mules with packs and water bottles and equipment hanging every which way, an older local woman approached them. She had the Slavic features of the native born of this area, and was old, as shown by the grey hair and wrinkled visage. She was strangely tattooed about the face and hands.

She walked right up to Quentin and pointing one gnarled finger at him kept repeating the words, "*Ettevaatust, Maa jumalad Tahad Sa. Ettevaatust! Ettevaatust!*" in her scratchy Estonian.

Needless to say, it was kind of freaking poor Quentin out who like all boys his age had no use for strange old women and like the rest of his father's team, had no idea what she was saying. One of the UN drivers, who by his visage was also a native, seemed quite upset by the encounter and started to say something to the old lady in rapid Estonian.

Quentin's Father stepped up, and pulling Quentin behind him, also started speaking, not to the old woman but to the UN driver who seemed most upset.

"What is she saying," he demanded of the driver.

The driver turned from the old woman to Quentin's father and replied, "This is a *Preestrinna*, how you say, seer or priestess, she is very old." He shot off a few more queries at the old woman who seemed to respond with just one or two words. "She serves the old gods. She is on a *palverännak*, on a... you say... search..., no pilgrimage. She says she was called to come here."

"Rubbish," Quentin's father said. The rest of his team watched the exchange with fascination, surreptitiously trying to take some photos and videos of the old woman. "What does she want with Quentin? Speak up man!" He demanded when it was obvious the driver was hesitant to say.

"She said, 'Beware, the god wants you,'" the driver finished, looking down at the ground.

"Rubbish, I say." And to his team, with his arm on Quentin's shoulders, "Come on, let's head in." And so Quentin, his father and the team headed into the National Park to traverse the mire, all the while the old woman's scratchy voice calling out behind them, "Ettevaatust, Ettevaatust!"

If this strange, otherworldly encounter upset Quentin, it didn't last for long for boys his age are resilient. And though it was strange by all accounts, no one on the team or Quentin's father supposed it was anything but the ravings of a mad old woman and was pushed to the back of the mind while more mundane matters took precedence.

The first few days were spent selecting a spot for setting up camp. As well as mapping the mire in the general vicinity of the newly formed temporary camp and setting up air and weather testing equipment. All the while Quentin was free to pursue his butterfly hunt, as long as he was back in camp by nightfall.

Quentin was having no luck in his search for the apparently elusive Clouded Apollo, though he had encountered many other varieties of species already in his collection, some of which he captured, many of which he ignored. With nearly 500 square kilometers of park and much of it wetlands, the plan was to move the camp at least twice to sample different areas. Quentin knew he'd have much opportunity to explore the park for his butterfly, so he was not feeling too discouraged.

After the first move deeper onto the mire a strange feeling took hold of the researchers, one of premonition perhaps, like something was going to happen. Not one of them correlated this feeling with the old woman's dire warning or spoke of it to another.

As the end of the first day in the new location approached, Quentin thought he spotted the Clouded Apollo and set to chase it with his net held out in front of him. It always seemed to stay just at the edge of his forward vision, always fluttering away just as he might reach it. Several times he felt the peat start to give way under his weight and had to move away quickly to avoid getting wet or worse. He made it back to the camp just as the sun set below the horizon determined to snatch his prey on the morrow.

That night a strange and unusual mist settled in and around the camp, which greeted Quentin and the team upon their rising the next morning.

"This is as thick as a London pea soup," Quentin's father commented. "Better stay close in to camp today," he told everyone. "We don't want to lose anyone," he finished with a laugh. Though disappointed, Quentin did as bid, and didn't leave the vicinity of the camp that day, instead watching videos stored on his iPad for as long as its battery held out.

That night, Quentin was woken when he thought he heard his name being called out. His Father was still asleep on the other side of the tent lightly snoring, so he dismissed it as a dream and went back to sleep. The others weren't so fortunate. Perhaps they also heard their names being called out, for in the morning the whole research team was nowhere to be found.

The fog was still thick and heavy around the camp. After calling out in loud voices for the missing team and searching the mire in proximity to the camp, Quentin's father felt it best if he went out to look for them. First, he notified the UN offices in Tallinn via satellite phone that his team had wandered off. He bade Quentin to stay in the tent until he returned, saying he shan't be too long and probably would find his team with some discovery or other. Dinosaur bones or something, most likely, he said.

Several hours passed and Quentin's father did not return. After much internal debate, an increasingly worried Quentin decided to call the UN offices himself and report this latest development. However, when Quentin tried to use the satellite phone he discovered the batteries were all but spent. His father must have left it on by accident. With no other means of electronic communication with the outside world, Quentin now had three choices as he saw it. One, he could hunker down and wait, someone might return. Two, he could attempt to hike out of the mire and find help. Three, he could go in search of his father.

As he stood staring out into the fog enshrouded mire, trying to decide the best course of action, the winds began to blow and the fog began to lift and dissipate. Soon the mire was clear all around him in every direction. This being the case, Quentin decided to go in search of his Father and headed off in the direction his father had gone earlier that day.

The mire seemed unusually quiet to Quentin. Though there were not many large animals, there were usually many birds and insects chittering and singing to one another. As always Quentin was careful to walk only where his experience told him the peat was thickest. Soon enough the camp was out of sight and Quentin was left with only mire in all directions. Suddenly the mire seemed to grab at Quentin's boot as he placed his foot, trying to suck him down. Quite shaken, Quentin vowed to go even slower and be more careful with where he stepped, even though the mire around him looked thick and firm.

Suddenly and unbidden, an image of the old woman rose up in his mind screeching the words ," *Ettevaatust! Ettevaatust!*, Beware!, Beware!"

Quentin's next step was his last, as the mire reached up and sucked him down completely, Clouded Apollos flittering furiously overhead. No one on the research team was ever found.

The End.

RHODA

The pounding on the door was a loud and insistent booming, rattling the window in its loose casement and the few glasses on the side cupboard. Pablo Fanque jumped up out of the lumpy bed, his only nightshirt flapping around him, careful of any noise that might give his presence away. He cautiously peered over the sill of the room's only exterior window to see what manner of loathsome bill collecting creature was hounding him today. After shading his eyes to the noon glare, he saw the tell-tale bun and glasses of his current landlady, Mrs. Whimple. He relaxed, somewhat gratified to see it was not the constables or someone intent on doing him worse harm. To Mrs. Whimple, he can always apply his gentlemanly charms and win the day with one of his signature smiles and perhaps a titillating story of yesteryear. Though, even that was growing thin on Mrs. Whimple, who just wanted her monthly room rent, now more than a week in arears.

Mrs. Whimple gave up in disgust, left off the pounding and went her way to bother some other unfortunate renter, or to call on her loathsome sister, Mrs. Jennings. When Pablo thought back to the unfortunate opportunity he had to meet Mrs. Jennings (widowed now, she always liked to add with a disturbing leer to any man of certain charms she may encounter), he shuddered internally, loathing to think of that leer directed at him.

Pablo caught himself ruminating about the unfortunate state of affairs life has left him in, bereft of coin and family and thinking marriage may be the only option. *It hasn't gotten that desperate yet,* he thought to himself, looking into his coin purse. There was just enough for a meal and a drink at his favorite tavern, The Hound and Horn, after which he planned on sauntering over to the Empire to see the house manager about a new show he, the great Pablo Fanque, was planning.

Not so many years ago, Pablo Fanque was one of London's most well-known circus owners, and a performer of some note. Pablo's troupe had comic tramps, acrobatics, jugglers, fire-eaters and a high wire walker, Pablo himself. So popular with the residents of London's west end, Pablo would book to sellout crowds in theaters like the Alhambra or the Empire, often times doing shows in both theaters on the same day.

During the heyday of his career, Pablo noted that the audiences of his shows were most rapt at any time someone was in personal danger. Oh, they loved the comic tramps running from the comic coppers. They enjoyed immensely the jugglers and the fire-eaters. But what got them going the most were the daredevil activities of the acrobats and his antics on the high wire. He also noted the audience was fairly beside themselves when young beauty was put in danger. When he added a young lady to the high wire act bravely risking her beauty to entertain, some in the audience nearly fainted. The applause, shouting and the tossing of flowers and coins seemed to go on indefinitely after such performances.

Finishing up his morning, well in Pablo's case, afternoon absolutions, Pablo donned his best long tailed coat, his least worn top hat, grabbed his favorite walking cane from the room's only chair and headed out the door, whistling all the way to the Hound and Horn. As noted earlier the Hound and Horn was Pablo's favorite, but not because of the first-rate meals, the intelligent conversation or the stunning décor, for it had none of these things. What the Hound and Horn did have was Grace. I don't mean Grace in the godly sense, I mean Grace of the magnificent bosoms who waited tables at the Hound and Horn and who always had a smile and kind word for Pablo and who bent down in just that perfect way.

One might wonder how did Pablo find himself in his current straits? A once great performer of some small accomplishment, popular with the ladies now reduced to near poverty, anonymity and stolen glances at Grace's bosoms? Pablo doesn't like to think of the reasons but in his mind, he places all the blame squarely on Abraham Saunders.

Not so long in the past London had as many as 350 circus shows preforming at one time. The large ones like Pablo's in theaters that charged up to 9p for entry. The smaller ones sometimes in outside venues or open-air theaters. Some even had aquatic shows. Needless to say, competition was fierce and every time a new show opened or a new act was contrived, the audiences moved like the ebb and flow of the ocean itself between theaters and shows, pulled by the new moon of novelty.

During one such seeming lull in Pablo's audience numbers, he chanced upon a man named Abraham Saunders who had an outdoor animal act. Not in itself unusual but in this particular case Abraham had a young lass in his show named Rhoda, who used to stick her dainty head into the lion's mouth very much in the literal way.

Abraham, as the show's own Master of Ceremonies, would build up the audience with stories of lion savagery while his aged and somewhat ratty looking lion would sit forlornly on a large overturned wooden box, chained to a stake in the ground lest some hunger forced him to look toward the tasty looking audience. Soon a young lady would seemingly rise up out of the audience and saunter over to the lion, all the while Abraham playing unawares. He would continue his stories of ghastly lion maimings while Rhoda, who knew the lion quite well, would coax its mouth open. All the while the audience was both terrified and rapt at what was about to happen next. All of them sure they were going to see Rhoda's headless corpse flop down to the stage. Often there would be shouting for the young lady to stop or for Abraham to pay attention to what was happening behind him, but to no avail. Sure enough, Rhoda would get the old Lion to open its mouth wide and in went her dainty little head.

When the audience realized it was all just part of the show, they went wild with enthusiasm for Rhoda and the lion, throwing what coins or foodstuffs they happened to have in their possession.

Pablo thought the whole spectacle was, well, spectacular and was soon enough convincing Abraham to join his circus at the Empire. After the small details were ironed out, it was decided that after a fortnight of practice, Abraham would get second billing and a split of the door take and he, the lion and Rhoda would join Pablo's troupe.

Sitting over drinks one evening in Pablo's large and well-appointed rooms, Abraham confessed to his new partner Pablo the trick of the act. Before the show Rhoda would liberally cover her neck in kerosene which the lion abhorred, thereby ensuring he would not close his mouth on young Rhoda's dainty neck and end the show, as it were.

This also gave Pablo an idea for his fire-eaters to enhance their act with fire-breathing. They could blow a fine mist of kerosene out of their mouths over an open flame, thereby appearing as if they were breathing fire.

Abraham, who had just returned from America told Pablo of a travelling circus he had seen there that had three rings. There were three different entertainments going on at once, on the same stage with a flamboyant ring master directing the audience where to gaze. Pablo thought it a novel idea to add to his show but decided to limit it to two acts at once. The fire-eaters who now also breathe fire would be on stage with Abraham and Rhoda. While Abraham gave his accounting of ghastly lion horrors, fire breathers would stand on either side and punctuate the worst atrocities with blowing flame.

Pablo and Abraham were both excited with the new acts and were convinced they were about to make a fortune. Pablo's whole troupe took a hiatus from performing because if the new acts were to open in just two weeks much careful practice would be needed. After several mishaps where the fire-eaters coughed and gagged on the kerosene, or spewed the atrocious fuel in all directions, just the right balance was struck and soon they were able to produce brilliant streams of flame. The blown flame would extend up to three feet, dependent on the amount of fuel held and the strength of the lungs in question.

One of Pablo's troupe, Maximillian, continued to practice in secret in order to get the longest flame possible even after Pablo told him he had it down well enough. Abraham and Rhoda didn't need to practice as their act was performed hundreds of times and they had the whole thing down pat, plus the lion got grumpy if forced to sit on his box on stage for too long. The only difference now was instead of standing amid a group of unorganized onlookers Rhoda would be seated in the audience.

On the night of the first new performance at the Empire every seat was sold out, with standing room only in the back. Now billed as:

Pablo Fanque's

Circus of Extraordinary Happenings

Starring Pablo Fanque and the Ferocious Beast

with Abraham Saunders

If Abraham cared his name was billed third even after the lion, he didn't show it possibly because he was about to make more money in one night than his old show made in an entire month. Plus, he'd never be rained on again while performing. That was how Abraham saw his change in fortune and the move into a large, indoor theater. No one stopped to consider how the lion might view now being on an indoor stage, bathed in lime-light with hundreds of people just a few feet away.

That first night, the lion's cage was dumped unceremoniously behind the stage curtains and off to one side to wait his turn at the limelight, as it were. In fact the Empire did have real lime-lights that illuminated the stage and Pablo in particular. The lion didn't like all the movement, activity and noise going on around him and the usual ratty blanket covering his cage seemed to be missing this night so all through the show the lion was becoming more and more agitated as he waited.

When it was finally time for Abraham and Rhoda's act, which was to be the grand finale, it was well over two hours into the show. Pablo took to the stage off to one side in his best costume and top hat, while a newly hired musical quartet played sinister sounding music from behind. During the oratorical build-up Pablo was subjecting the audience to, half the stage was closed off behind the curtain while stage hands moved the lion's box into place. The flame-breathers took their positions at the front of the stage with mouth's full of kerosene. Finally, Abraham led the lion out of his cage and up onto the box while Rhoda had been seated all night long acting as part of the audience.

The rest of the curtain rose to the accompanying gasps of the audience as Abraham began his bone-chilling tales of the capture of the fearsome beast sitting just behind him and the flame breathers breathed fire out toward the audience. Soon, Rhoda rose from the audience and made her way on the stage seemingly without Abraham noticing. The audience, to whom this was all new, tried vainly to get Abraham to notice the young girl as she creeped behind the flame breathers and toward the increasingly agitated lion.

Just as Rhoda moved behind Maximillian, the lion finally remembered he was king of the forest and after jumping down from the box gave out a spectacular roar, which caused several ladies in the audience to scream in fright and several men jump up ready to do battle with the beast, fists raised. It also caused Maximillian to jerk his head around toward the unexpected noise and blow out his flame at Rhoda, to a breathtaking five feet, a world record no doubt. Rhoda, who having had her neck coated in the same noxious fuel so the lion wouldn't be tempted to snip her little head off, immediately and suddenly burst into flame.

That was the end of Pablo Fanque's circus, though no one could say that it wasn't truly extraordinary.

The End.

Susan

Mrs. Bowers was a woman who liked to have things just so. Every painting was hung with particular care, every lace doily perfectly centered, every lamp and table well dusted. This striding for perfection invaded every facet of Mrs. Bowers outlook on life. Every bush and flower in her meticulously manicured lawn was symmetrical. Every one of her hats matched perfectly with every one of her outfits.

She was particularly conscious of this need when it came to her small family. Their place in the social pecking order of their small community secure. Her husband was of a respectable family and held a respectable job. He drove his Cadillac home every evening from the office promptly on time and Mrs. Bowers had supper on the table at half past six. Every Saturday he took on chores around the house and yard and every Sunday after church they went for a country drive and often visited his mother in the home. Whatever Mr. Bowers thought of all this order, he kept securely to himself.

To Mrs. Bowers their life couldn't have been more perfect even down to their one and only child, Susan.

Susan was taught from infancy to be compliant to her mother's wishes. It's not that Mrs. Bowers was cruel or unloving, she loved her family deeply and was a kind, generous woman in her way, she just wanted her family to be…, well, perfect. Mrs. Bowers was mortified of the idea of being embarrassed in public and her life was fine-tuned to avoid just that.

By the time Susan was four she knew exactly how to act. Susan was always clean and well dressed. Her room was always picked up and in order. The books were always placed back on the shelves, the toys in the box and the clothes and shoes in the closet. Susan had impeccable manners. In fact, Mrs. Bower's neighbors always commented on how well-behaved Susan was, making Mrs. Bowers very satisfied.

When it so happened that a new family moved in down the street and it was found out they also had a daughter the same age as Susan Mrs. Bowers felt a momentary twinge. This was the first unaccounted episode to happen to Mrs. Bowers life in many years. Setting aside her small trepidation Mrs. Bowers proceeded to bake the new neighbors a three-layer vanilla cake with strawberry frosting, planning on walking it over there on Sunday after church with her perfect little family in tow. Welcoming new neighbors was what one did, in polite society.

Though Susan loved vanilla cake and strawberry frosting, she knew from past experience even if the new neighbors offered, she wasn't allowed to have a piece. A 'no, thank you' was the response Mrs. Bowers expected Susan to make.

Sunday came and the carefully frosted cake was securely ensconced on the plastic Avon covered cake plate with Mrs. Bowers name securely taped to the bottom, lest said cake plate not be returned.

The arm in arm walk to the new neighbors was a pleasant stroll through a well-known world. Here and there the Bowers would wave and say hello to any neighbor who happened to be outside. Upon arriving at the home of the new neighbors, Mrs. Bowers was gratified to see nothing looked out of place since the Kinsey's had moved out. No moving boxes littered the fine front lawn, no old junkers were parked in the driveway and the white lace curtains were hung on the windows with care.

"Maybe you'll make a new friend, Susan," Mrs. Bowers said. "Wouldn't that be nice, dear?"

"Yes mother, it would," Susan replied meekly. Though Susan had many acquaintances, true friends were hard to make and keep considering her mother's vetting process. If the whole family wasn't perfect, by Mrs. Bowers standards, they didn't pass muster.

"She's too loud, dear." Her mother would say, or "her parents are separated, dear," when Susan would ask about having someone over, or ask to go over to someone's house.

Momentarily after Mr. Bowers rang the doorbell a well-kept woman of youngish years answered the door. Mrs. Bowers introduced them all and finagled an invitation inside in order to be able to check things out more closely. You can't be too careful after all.

The new neighbor turned out to be one Marcia Porter recently divorced and new to the Bower's small town. Even more scandalously, Ms. Porter was a writer for a certain woman's fiction magazine and worked from home. Her daughter, who came down stairs to see what was going on, was introduced as Jennifer. And indeed it was discovered Jennifer was also eight years old like Susan.

Now sensing looming danger, Mrs. Bowers tried to extricate them all from the hornet's nest of imperfection. Imagine, divorced and a writer of fictional smut. Having no imagination for such things, Mrs. Bowers didn't understand ladies' fiction regarding love and sex or many other things.

"Oh my look at the time, we really need to get going." She said glancing at her watch.

"Don't be silly," Ms. Porter replied kindly, "after making this beautiful cake you have to stay and have a piece, I insist. I'll just put the tea on." Off into the kitchen she went saying, "Jennifer, bring them all along."

Susan was becoming hopeful that maybe there would be a piece of cake involved in today. Mr. Bower looked to his wife to gauge which direction he should head. Truth be told, Mrs. Bowers wasn't sure what to do. It would be the epitome of rudeness to leave now, but to defer and stay could be an uncomfortable beginning to trouble.

Jennifer grabbed Susan's hand and dragged her off into the kitchen, with her parents having no choice but to follow.

The next week Ms. Porter invited Susan for dinner and a sleep over, via an excited invite orally repeated by Jennifer. Normally, Mrs. Bowers would not allow Susan to go under any circumstances but having just been notified by the home that Mr. Bower's mother had a stroke and they were needed at once she was in a tight spot. As they had no regular sitter and there being no one else able to look after Susan, Mrs. Bowers reluctantly acquiesced, making the best of a worst-case scenario.

Mrs. Bowers consoled herself with the thought, 'what could one time possibly hurt?' But as her mother-in-law needed more and more, Mrs. Bowers was pulled from home more often and had to rely on Ms. Porter's willingness to look after Susan when there was no other option available. Susan and Jennifer became fast friends. Ms. Porter was thrilled to have Susan's polite, respectful and well-mannered influence on Jennifer. But as Mrs. Bowers feared, Jennifer also influenced Susan.

Jennifer was eight and her mother was often distracted with work. When she wanted her way she knew exactly how to get it. If pleading and reasoning didn't work on her mother, throwing a tantrum often did.

"But only do it as a last resort," Jennifer wisely advised Susan. "Fall down on the floor and hold your breath. You might want to kick and scream if that doesn't work. Even your mother will give in. Mine does, but don't push it too far or you will just end up getting punished."

Susan heard all this with disbelief. She couldn't imagine throwing a tantrum in front of her mother. She couldn't imagine her mother ever giving in to anything. Even when she witnessed it work on Jennifer's mother one evening, she couldn't imagine doing it herself.

But then one evening Jennifer and her mom invited Susan to go with them to the movies even though it was a school night. Mrs. Bowers had just got back home in time to pick Susan up from school and Mr. Bower had called to apologize and say he had to work late for his boss. Mrs. Bowers was tired and disheveled. Something that could almost never be said of her.

"Absolutely not." Mrs. Bowers said, when Susan carefully broached the subject over supper of heated up leftovers, more evidence of Mrs. Bower's spiral as she never served leftovers.

"Why?" Susan demanded with a particular agitated tone. "I want to go."

"What you are going to do, young lady, is finish your supper, clean up the table and then go to your room and do your homework." Mrs. Bowers answered, as close to an angry tone as she ever had. If Susan had picked up on the clues of exactly how close Mrs. Bowers was to losing her temper she would have saved her fight for another issue. An epic grounding was sure to follow, but as Susan had never seen her mother lose her temper, she didn't know the warning signs.

Susan scraped her chair back in a huff, threw herself onto the divan next to the wall and proceeded to throw a tantrum like the Bower house had never seen or imagined. There was arm flailing, there were tears, there was yelling. Mrs. Bowers was momentarily stunned.

"Susan!" She demanded. "What on Earth? Stop that at once!"

But poor Susan couldn't stop. Unknown at the time Susan had been born with an enlarged heart, something not usually seen without special scans. Poor Susan's fit had turned real, with the flailing and coughing and gasping for air.

It was only pure luck and the quiet and ordinary events of Susan's home life that had ensured her survival this long. Too much excitement would be the end of poor Susan.

And this tantrum would be her first and last.

The End.

TITUS

The backhanded smack sent her flying onto the frayed couch of the small three-room apartment on the second floor of an aging four story in Dublin's Finglas neighborhood. Since his earliest years Titus had witnessed many such scenes between his parents. Titus' father had a particular taste for Jamesons (or any whiskey he could get, really). When he wasn't able to drink he was easily enraged. With that kind of father and a mousy terrified mother, Titus' eleven years have been filled with fear and trepidation. As Titus has been growing older some of that fear has been coalescing into anger and determination. Any love or respect he once had for his old man has long since dissipated. His mother he loved even more and longed to be able to protect and support her.

But what can an eleven-year-old boy do?

He knew his father would soon storm out of the apartment in a rage and slamming the door behind him mutter curses all the way down the stairs, presumably in search of a drink. Titus had seen it many times. His mother would barricade herself in the small, molding bathroom, crying until she finally settled down enough to come out. Then it seems she would remember Titus and calling him over to her, she would sit him on her lap on the old couch and try to console his fear.

"He's not a bad man," she would say. Titus never had any reply. Titus was too young to understand the pressures of adults or why his mother didn't leave his father.

He turned and went into the small kitchen to find something for supper to quell his growing hunger hearing the front door slam just as Titus knew it would, with his father's departure. Pulling the chair over and reaching up to the top of the refrigerator he found that the loaf of store bought bread was a little moldy, but usable. There was one tin of sardines in the little cabinet next to the sink. He trimmed the bread and made himself and his mother a sandwich, served on one of the small plates that somehow managed to survive the many fights between his parents. When his father was really, really mad, he took to smashing things in the apartment, one-time smashing plate after plate on the floor. He almost put one of his mother's eyes out with a shard of flying porcelain and leaving her brow bloody.

That time Titus cowered in the corner watching, terrified. His father stayed away for three days after that and Titus had wished he would never come back.

Titus quick survey of the kitchen showed little else to eat and he knew he needed to go out. Titus had taken to scouring the neighborhood for things to take and bring home. Vegetables and fruit from vendors or from the market on the corner, loaves of bread cooling on window sills or from the baker's display. One time even he scored a whole ham when the butcher's assistant left the back door open to the alley that he quickly ran home with. They ate for many days on that. Neither his mother nor his father asked where these things came from.

Occasionally his father found work on the docks or loading and unloading trucks and would come home drunk from the pub with money in his pocket. Titus would sneak into his parent's room and rummage through his inebriated father's pockets, taking the coin he could find and then purchase much needed things for him and his mother. But that had not happened for a while.

Titus gobbled down his sandwich, left the other on the table covered with a cloth, and slipped out of the apartment while his mother was still in the bathroom.

Recently, he had been having some trouble with a group of older boys in the area and was being particularly cautious. Titus was good at being cautious. The fact that he hadn't been caught pilfering yet was a testament to his ability. He was patient, he could wait for just the right moment to grab and run. Had he been from a higher class, with more refined tastes, he might have made an excellent cat burglar.

Dublin in the early seventies was not a particularly pleasant place. The Blacks and Browns patrolling the streets with guns out in the open, the IRA blowing things up seemingly at random, the unemployment, the poverty and hunger. A boy with Titus's disadvantages seemingly had no hope for a bright future.

Titus carefully made his way out of his neighborhood, ever watchful for trouble and scampered into a more prosperous part of the city. He had overheard a show on the telly about a row of shops he wanted to check out that weren't too far away, hoping for better pickings. As he made his way past the cleaner and better kept row houses and small parks, he also noticed several 'An Post' trucks making deliveries of small packages to people's homes. Titus imagined all sorts of things in those brown, paper wrapped boxes. He imagined people sending other people puddings and boxes of fruit or new clothes and shoes -things Titus deserved but had no one to provide.

Titus was ever careful to avoid attention while scouting out the new row of shops he found though people noticed an unkempt boy in ratty looking, ill-fitting clothes milling about, particularly shopkeepers who always kept a keen eye out for such things. Titus saw several discouraging looks made his way while he tried to project a look of innocent wonder. These shops and these people were the most prosperous Titus had encountered so far, but he had no use for jewelry or fancy imported candles and the shops that did look promising had one or more keen eyed watchers meant to discourage such activities as was in Titus' mind.

He decided to check out the alley behind the shops to see of any of these fancy places threw needful things out or if anyone had left a door open. But Titus wasn't the first or only one with the same thought, and this alley already had a gleaner who looked threateningly at Titus. Discouraged, Titus turned for his own neighborhood and his usual haunts.

On the way back he saw an interesting thing happen. He noticed the group of older boys he had been accosted by earlier in the week, skulking through the yards down the street. Titus quickly hid behind some cans hoping they hadn't seen him in order to watch. While several of the boys had positioned themselves apparently as look outs, one boy ran up onto a porch and snatched a medium sized brown package from in front of the door and skedaddled off down the road with his friends following. Titus was awed by the audacity and watched intently to see if chase was to be given by an enraged homeowner or if a mean dog was to be released to do its fearsome savagery. None was forthcoming. Not a peep was heard from the house that was just pilfered or for that matter from any of the neighbors.

A whole new world of larceny opened up before Titus.

Titus became very good at the porch snatch and grab, as he thought of it. He went out early in the morning before his mother was up to watch a series of selected porches. When he saw both man and woman leave, he'd keep a mental note of a possibly daytime empty home. If he later encountered one of the many 'An Post' trucks crisscrossing the city making deliveries he would know if a porch was safe to run up to and make the snatch.

The trick was finding a safe place to open the pilfered package away from the prying eyes of suspicious coppers or other adults. He became well acquainted with the back alleyways and hidden drives of Belfast, where he'd open his ill-gotten gifts. He was also very wary of the group of older boys and stayed under their radar as much as possible.

Though he never got much in the way of food, except for the occasional baked good, Titus acquired many useful things for himself and his mother, sweaters and coats, slippers and shoes, some fit, some did not. What he couldn't use he left in the alleys for others to find.   One time in a particularly heavy box he found a complete set of Mark Twain books.

Come mid-July of 1972 Titus was on school break and had ample time to do his hunting. Things at home were looking well provisioned.   Titus father hadn't been home in several weeks and Titus' mother seemed almost content, which made Titus almost happy.

On that July 21st, Titus rose early, pulled on a relatively new suit of clothes he 'found' last week, complete with tie, and set out into his Belfast neighborhood. Titus learned that the better he dressed the less suspicious he seemed to people. He had even revisited that row of upscale shops and was able to pilfer several great things without notice.

After a particularly sparse day of hunting, Titus found himself near the middle of Belfast at around 2 'clock in the afternoon. The day seemed unusually busy and Titus was giving up hope of any good things today. Just as he turned a corner he witnessed a couple of men in a plain looking car drop a brown paper wrapped package off in front of a small, busy pub, before the car sped away down the street. Titus quickly ran over and snatching up the package, ran around the corner and into the alley. The little package was really quite heavy so Titus was hopeful for good things.

That day in Belfast more than 130 people were seriously injured in a series of IRA bombings that would later be known as 'Bloody Friday.' Though unaccredited, Titus had saved the many people in the pub and other passerbys from serious injury or death.

Titus had opened the package deep in the back of an alley away from pedestrians and crowded shops.

When that particular bomb blew up that day, only one small boy was killed by it and not all of his bits and pieces were recovered or identified.

The End.

UNA

It was about three in the afternoon when my door flew open and the dame walked in. I was dozin' off at my desk after having maybe one too many at lunch. Cases had been kinda sparse lately, see what I mean? She was a nice lookin' one in her way but was obviously very upset.

"Mr. Nolan?" she inquired.

"Yeahs," I said, tryin' to straighten my tie and find out where my cigar had fallen to. "Whose askin?"

"I need to hire you. What do you charge?" At least it was right down to business. Now usually with the pretty ones I like to take my time. Maybe see where it can go, see what I mean? I let her stand there wringing her hands while I looked her up and down. Nice hat, nice shoes, but not the best. In my line of work you get an eye for these things. Not too bad off I figures but not really flush either.

"Depends," I says. "Am I gonna get shot at," I asks, spotting my cigar under the desk. It must have rolled off onto the floor when I was snoozing.

"Shot at? Do people usually shoot at you, Mr. Nolan, Mr. Nolan?" She said as I had disappeared under my desk to retrieve my cigar.

"No, not usually," I answered around my recovered cigar, straightening up. I don't smoke, 'em, just like to chew on the end. "But it has happened. I don't like it." I added.

The dame paused for a second. "My Una is missing," she said quietly. "May I sit?"

I motioned to the only other chair in the office, a none too sturdy and uncomfortable wooden job I picked up off the sidewalk. I don't want anyone too comfortable. She took off her raincoat and laid it over the back of the chair. It was still wet from the rain we've been having for the last week and then sat precariously on the edge of the chair.

"Your what is missing," I asked with raised eyebrows, not sure I heard her all the way.

"My daughter, her name is Una? I haven't seen her in three days." She stopped to wipe a tear from one eye.

A simple missing person then, I thought. Probably ran off with a lover or boyfriend. Not too bad a gig, all in all. Better than, say a cheating spouse I figures, see what I mean?

"How old is your daughter, Mrs....?" I asked.

"I'm Natalie Hayle, Mr. Nolan, and my daughter will be eight years old next week."

"Eight?" I verified, thinking and chewing furiously now, my fingers tapping on the arm of my chair. This is gonna be harder than I thought. I don't wanna get involved with any child snatching gangs, if there was one operating here. I hadn't heard a peep. That too was worrying, see what I mean?

"Have you been to the police?" I asked. "I have a buddy downtown helps me out once in a while, let me find his card." I said rummaging through all the crap on my desk. I found it near the bottom of a pile with some kind of stain on it, ketchup maybe. "Detective John Mallory at the 7th. A mick... er an Irishman, but pretty solid for all of that." I finished proffering the card to her.

She looked at the card in my outreached hand but didn't take it.

"At the 7th?" she inquired.

"The 7th precinct, it's down on, well 7th Ave," I said with a wave of my hand toward the window.

"The police can't help me," she paused, "or won't help me," she finished sadly. "Do you know how many children go missing in this city every year, Mr. Nolan?"

Unfortunately, I did. Kids were snatched for a variety of reasons, few of them pleasant to think about.

"No ransom demands?" I asked knowing the answer already from experience. Few are ever kidnapped for something as simple as money.

"No, nothing, why, do you think she was kidnapped?" she asked breathlessly, putting one hand to her mouth.

"Probably not, Mrs. Nolan. Not if you haven't heard anything already." I hate missing kid cases. They hardly ever end well. I did some more searching of my desk and came up with a pen and paper to take notes. Guess I was gonna take the case after all, see what I mean?

"Tell me the story from the beginning, where you live, where..., Una is it? goes to school and what happened out of the ordinary in the days leading up to her disappearance. Today is Thursday, so say from last weekend."

She started hesitantly, but with a few small probing questions I got to hear the whole story. Una was almost eight but was exceptionally talented and bright, apparently. She was very slight in build, even for an eight-year-old Mrs. Hayle told me, even often being mistaken for a boy of four or five. There seemed to be nothing out of the ordinary in their lives in the past week.

"Could she have run away?" I asked, "or is there a Mr. Hayle who might have taken her?"

"Una's father passed several years ago and she would never have run away. She was... is a very happy child. Always laughing and playing. She loved school and has many friends there."

I handed her another sheet of paper. "Write down all the information I need to get started, school address, friend's names, other relatives, anyone I could speak to or any places I can check out. And, I need a photo."

After a few minutes of furious writing, she handed it all to me taking a photo out of her purse, with a glimmer of tears in her eyes.

"Thank you, Mr. Nolan. I can't tell you how relieved I am that someone will be helping us. Una is all I have now." She paused for a moment, possibly reminiscing about something. "Oh, you never told me what you charge," she finished.

"In a case like this usually just expenses which should be minimal, I hope. I keep receipts. After I find your Una," I said motioning to the photo, "we will talk about the rest."

After she left I got up and I put on my hat, my raincoat and found my umbrella. It was still raining and at this rate we were all gonna float away. I hated pounding the pavement in the rain, but my wheels were in the shop, see what I mean? I figure I'd start with the school and then the neighbors. Also, I would head down toward the docks and nose around for what I could hear about any organized groups working the city.

Someone always knows something or so I thought, but this time there was almost nothing to go on after two days spent talking and questioning those who knew Una and her mother. I got soaked but little else. I finally asked my buddy down in the 7th what he could find out. It seems the coppers did some asking around also but came up with nothing as well.

"What do you hear about a gang of snatchers working the city, then?" I asked him, perched on the edge of his desk, chewing on my cigar. The look on his face told me if there was one it was news to him.

"If you've heard of something, you better spill it", he said, looking up and glowering at me. So, there was nothing there, I thought to myself. If there was they'd been quiet as mice.

"Seems like this kid just upped and disappeared, see what I mean?" I said.

"Kids don't just disappear." He grumbled. Ordinarily I would agree, but usually there was something to go on.

"What'd you think about the kid's mother, think she coulda done her in," he asked me. I had to stop and ponder. She sure didn't seem the type but hey, if life has taught me anything, it's that you just never know. I told him as much.

"If we don't at least find the body we don't have anything to go on," he said shaking his head.

"With all this rain she coulda just washed down a storm drain," I joked sadly.

"Well, if she did, the alligators had for her then."

The End.

VICTOR

"Now arriving Amtrak train number 68 from Montreal. Next stop Albany-Rensellear. Alllllllll Aboard," the old-time Amtrak agent spoke into the PA system of the small train station in upstate NY, out into the milling crowd of afternoon travelers. All were heading downstate, most into the city. Victor squealed with delight as the blue and silver train pulled into the station with a continuous tooting of its horn.

"Mom, Mom, here it is. C'mon, let's go out," Victor said, dodging through the crowd of people from the window where he had been on watch. Some were hugging loved ones goodbye while others were pulling on luggage toward the doors. When Victor reached her he pulled on her hand to pull her up and led her outside.

Victor loved trains, always had. His parents occasionally brought him to the station to watch them come and go. The passenger trains that stopped for travelers north or south, the long freight trains that whizzed by the terminal, blowing their horns furiously or the excursion trains that originated here, with their double-decker dome cars that ran daily into the Adirondacks. Victor loved them all.

Once the people all boarded, and the train pulled out of the station with its bell ringing to resume its journey, Victor and his mom turned to go back into the station and visit the gift shop, Victor happy as a lark.

As they had been here many times, Victor immediately noticed the new posters advertising a special Christmas time train ride, 'The Polar Express', Victor almost fainted with excitement. The Polar Express was Victor's favorite movie, and he had seen it at least a bazillion times. Imagine, the real Polar Express right here! Victor couldn't contain himself, he whooped and danced in circles, pointing up to the posters. He almost peed his pants.

"Mom!" He managed to shout out just once.

The gift shop attendant also turned out to be the excursion train ticket agent, who couldn't help but notice Victor's excitement. "Whoa there, buddy... you're gonna burst something," he said laughing. "You wanna go to the North Pole and see Santa this year?"

Victor managed another strangled, "Mom!" the excitement deep in his eyes. Now also looking at the posters, Victor's mom said, "It looks just like your favorite movie, Vic. Should we do it?" And turning to the agent said, "can you tell us about the ride?"

"Gladly," the agent responded obviously enjoying the telling. "The Polar Express departs the station twice a night starting the night after Thanksgiving and every night until the day before Christmas Eve. As you board the 'Conductor' guides you to your seats and punches the special 'Golden Ticket'. As the train travels up to the North Pole, dancing and singing 'Chefs' serve everyone hot chocolate and cookies. Once the train pulls into the North Pole station Santa and all his Elves board the train for the ride back. Along the way the Elves lead everyone in caroling and Santa gives a special gift to every child."

"Mom! It's the real train like in the movie! Can we go?"

Arrangements were made, a date was chosen and the fairly expensive tickets purchased for the second of the evenings ride on the night before Christmas Eve.

Today's trip was one of the most unbelievable trips to the train station Victor had ever made. Imagine, the real Polar Express and Victor was going! Christmas this year was gonna be the best ever!

That night when Victor's dad got home from work, Victor was fairly bursting with the news of the Polar Express. He had kept a sharp eye out the window all day for his dad's car to pull into the driveway. As soon as he saw it he gave out a loud 'Whoop!" and ran to the door and flung it open.

"Dad, Dad!" he yelled so furiously Victor's dad thought something must be terribly wrong and ran into the house. When his dad spied Victor's mom's hugely smiling face behind the boy, he felt reassured. "What is it, son?" his dad asked.

"We are going on the Polar Express! We saw it today at the train station and the guy said it goes to the North Pole and Santa will give me a present and there will be hot chocolate and elves and cookies. It's real dad. It's all real!" Victor blurted out so fast many an auctioneer would be jealous.

"Wow, Vic that sounds great," he said looking inquiringly at Victor's mom.

"It's true, Vic's got it right. We are all going to the North Pole on the Polar Express," she said handing the tickets and brochure to her husband.

"Wow", is all he could think to say.

The days leading up to the big train ride seemed to last twice as long as normal for Victor. All he could think about was the Polar Express. He watched and re-watched the movie as many times as his parents would allow him and had an endless stream of questions. "What kind of cookies will we have?" he wondered. "How old are the elves?" he asked. "Will Santa give everyone a silver bell, like in the movie?" he inquired hopefully. "Will I get to keep the golden ticket?" and on and on.

Finally the day of the train ride arrived and right on time (no pun intended).

The traffic going into and coming out of the station in this small upstate New York city was heavily congested. This train station and the streets around it were never designed to accommodate the cars for the1600 people the two nightly Polar Express rides carried. By the time they managed to park Victor feared they were going to be too late to catch the train.

As soon as his dad stopped the car in the spot Victor, who was clad in his best PJ's (that's how you dress for the Polar Express) burst out of it and ran toward the waiting train which could be seen and heard loudly idling on the other side of the station. It's long passenger cars decorated gaily for the trip north.

"Victor!" He heard his dad yell. His response was not to slow or stop but to yell back, "Come on!" all good sense having run from his head like the water running over Niagara Falls in his excitement.

Now though this is a smaller station as train stations go, it was still heavily used. There were no fewer than five tracks on which trains could travel, and did so regularly.

As he ran up to the track side of the building Victor saw many groups of people waiting on the siding to board the Polar Express, all standing obediently behind the yellow line all excited and ready to go. The train looked magical to Victor, who knew deep in his young bones that he needed a closer look.

Without so much as a second thought Victor darted out in front of the still train and around the engine to the other side onto the adjoining tracks. He had never been so close to the large and powerful engine or had this view of the long, snaking train of cars. He was totally and completely enthralled.

On that cold Christmas Eve's eve, an excited young boy named Victor failed to realize his terrible danger. Just then, a heavily laden freight train was approaching the station from the other direction and though the engineer was keeping a sharp eye out and progressing slowly past the busy passenger station, his horn tooting all the while, he never could have seen the small still figure of the young boy standing on the tracks, who was oblivious to everything going on around him.

It was too late for Victor when he finally realized his error and turned around just in time to see the blinding lights of the behemoth that was bearing inexorably upon him, to his ultimate doom.

There was no Polar express for anyone else the remainder of that year.

The End.

Winnie

I don't know if her parents thought it would be some kind of lark to name their first daughter after the city she was born in, or if it was just out of some sort of absurd idiocy. Children should never be named cutesy little names to amuse their parents. If your last name is Bond, please do not name your child James. If your last name is Robbins, don't name your son Christopher. If your last name is Mayonnaise, don't name your kid Hellmans. We've all met them, the Rainbow Auroras and the Bluebell Madonnas of the world. The poor things handicapped right out of the the gate.

Winnipeg Tremblay was a shy little thing, quiet and self-effacing. The kind of girl you might completely overlook even if she was in the same room with you. In fact, many times her teachers would completely miss her when they took attendance, so even though she never missed a day of school, she had an awful attendance record.

"Winnie? Winnie? Winnipeg?" The teacher would ask, finally looking up from the ledger and even though little Winnie would whisper as loud as she could 'here' and even raised her little hand, she would be overlooked. Being seated behind that big brute and bully of a boy, Josh Gagnon didn't help. Poor Winnie couldn't even see around him and often sat down on the floor under her desk in order to see the chalkboard from between his legs.

She was so quiet she easily slipped into and out of places totally unnoticed, even if she stopped and said 'hello' to whomever else was present. Several times the bus driver drove all the way back to the garage before he noticed little Winnie still on the bus when he started to sweep.

But Winnie was like every other girl in her 3rd grade class in many ways. She liked reading but she didn't like fractions, she had trouble with her cursive 'G' and excelled at geography. Winnie liked princesses and dogs, liked to wear her hair in pony tails and her favorite color was yellow. She went to everyone's birthday parties, even though she was hardly ever invited. She gave everyone in the class a valentine even that horrible Josh Gagnon. She offered to share her homework, which was always completed on-time. She laughed when one of her classmates said a funny thing and cried just a little when she saw a smushed squirrel in the road.

Now Winnie's parents weren't *bad* parents, just distracted a bit. Winnie was so quiet and so well behaved even they didn't always know she was nearby and, in their defense, they were both busy professionals. So as the seasons had passed Winnie largely made her own way through childhood.

Speaking of seasons, Winnie's favorite was winter and there was a lot of winter in Manitoba. One day you might go to bed after a pleasantly warm fall day and wake up in a winter wonderland. In Manitoba winter always came on in full force, like a D-Day invasion, and in turn, it left only in little itty, bitty steps, spring fighting it for every inch of ground and new bud.

One of the reasons Winnie loved winter was because she loved to ice fish. She loved ice fishing even more than her father who was the one who taught her how in the first place. Her father would shake her awake early in the morning, even before the sun has completely woke, bundle her up in her warmest coat, boots, mittens and hat and off they would go to the frozen river or lake to set out their tip-ups.

Winnie and her father would trudge down the bank with all their paraphernalia, the ice saw, the bait bucket, the collapsible stools and all the stuff they needed to build a fire and make hot chocolate and if they were gonna be there long enough or in the afternoon, hotdogs.

After finding a suitable spot on the ice Winnie's father would cut two or three holes and help Winnie bait and setup the tip-ups with their bright orange flags just ready to pop up at the first feel of a tug on the line. Then they would retreat to the nearest spot on the bank, set their little camp fire and stools and Winnie's father would make the hot chocolate served steaming in bright white Styrofoam cups. There would always be sticky cinnamon rolls too, that her mother baked the previous night and sent along with them, wrapped in cloth napkins. It was a cold, but wonderful time.

Now another thing should be said about the ice in Manitoba. Ice formed quickly on the water in this Canadian Province, the bitter cold artic jet stream saw to that. A still lake or pond might form four to five inches of ice in the deep cold winter night. There were always little dashes out to the tip-ups being made to keep the ice in the holes loosened, in case a big fish had to be pulled up through one. Pulled up and released, for Winnie wouldn't have it any other way.

After a successful morning of ice fishing, and after exclamations of frozen toes and cold noses and with much rubbing of hands together, everything would be packed back up and loaded back into the car with the heater blasting for Winnie and her Father.

It just so happened that this autumn, Winnie's teacher was hosting a classroom contest, the winners of which would be invited to her home in the week before Christmas for sledding, ice skating and a winter cookout. Winnie's teacher distributed colored notecards to tape on everyone's desk and on these cards the teacher would make a mark every time the student in question accomplished something good. Hand raised and question answered equaled a mark. Homework turned in on time equaled a mark. B or better on a test equaled a mark. Perfect attendance every week equaled a mark. Desk and surrounding area left clean and neat at the end of the day equaled a mark. The whole class was very excited with the idea of all of this and anxious to make their marks.

Winnie earned an admirable number of marks on her yellow note card, as many as anyone, in fact. But she noticed that Josh, sitting directly in front of her, wasn't earning very many and was obviously becoming sad about it as the end of the contest approached. Feeling sorry for him, every time Winnie passed by Josh's desk she would surreptitiously take her pencil and add a mark onto Josh's card. No one noticed, not even Josh.

After collecting up the cards at the end of the contest period and adding up all the marks, I'm sure Winnie's teacher was surprised that Josh had accumulated so many marks. Since it had always been her intention to invite everyone in the class anyway, as was only right, she gave it no never mind.

Finally, the big day came. Winnie was very particular that day about her attire. She insisted to her mother that she wear only her best winter garb, the boots with the faux fur lining, the big fluffy yellow ski jacket and the brown mittens with the faux fur ruffle. Added to all this was her favorite yellow scarf sent last Christmas from her grandmother, and the rainbow-colored hat with the long top with the big fuzzy ball at the very tip.

When Winnie was dropped off at the teacher's home, everything was as festive as could be. Christmas lights were gaily strung over bushes and trees, paper bag lights were used to line the shoveled path into the back yard where a brightly decorated tent was set up with tables and chairs and electric heaters and tables overflowing with bowls of chips and salads and chocolates and row upon row of soft drinks. Several enclosed fire pits were in the yard and at least two grills going full strength. There were gales of laughter and screams of joy coming from several groups of children already there, from around the sledding hill or from around the snowman building area. Here and there groups of children were dotted with adults, some of the parents who were enjoying themselves just as much. Winnie's parents were too busy to attend.

After Winnie made her presence known to her teacher, which took much tugging on the coat of and jumping up and down, she headed over to the sledding hill. It was massively tall in Winnie's eyes and excitement surged through her in anticipation of hurtling down its steep slopes.

About 20 feet out from the bottom of the hill was a nice sized pond shoveled off for ice skating but no one had yet ventured out onto it. As the freshly fallen snow was still soft, the hurtling sleds all stopped well short of the pond itself.

There was a small break in the action on the hill as the adult in charge had to take a break. While Winnie was dutifully trudging up the slippery hill to reach its summit and take her turn on a sled, unbeknownst to anyone, Josh the aforementioned bully whom Winnie herself made sure was present, was liberally pouring water all over the ground on the sled run, in order to increase the distance and speed once it froze over.

Winnie was the first to be loaded onto a sled when the adult in charge returned, steaming hot chocolate cup in hand. "You ready to fly down this hill, young lady?" he asked. Winnie's hat tail swayed wildly as she shook her head in an excited affirmative. "Hang on tight!" he yelled as he gave a push to the back of Winnie's sled.

Winnie fairly flew down the sledding hill, happy screams trailing out behind her like invisible streamers. As she reached the bottom and struck the newly formed ice, Winnie's sled hurtled onward toward the waiting pond, not slowing even a bit. No one but Josh was paying the least bit of attention as Winnie's sled crashed over the ice of the pond and out onto the very weakest part of the ice, the middle. The blades of the old wooden sled cut deep grooves into the ice, causing it to crack. The sled stopped achingly fast as it ground into the ice, throwing Winnie several feet up and out onto the ice with a sickening crack.

As Winnie was thrown onto and through the ice, it reformed quickly over her and within a few hours Winnie was embedded completely in the frozen water of the pond, forever gazing skyward.

The End.

XERXES

There are few things more wholesome for a child than to be raised on a farm with the clean country air, the wide-open spaces for playing and running, the inspiring vistas of mountain and sky. Farm living fosters an appreciation and an affinity for nature. The link between earth and life is apparent every day. The cycle of birth and death and of sowing and reaping fosters a gratitude for hard work that is well rewarded, along with a belief of everything in its own time.

A farm life can be a tough life though, being primarily dependent on the bounty of nature. Droughts, floods, infestations, sickness, disease and death all can take a toll. There can be as many bad years as good years, but typically the good years are very good, while the bad teach one a certain stoicism about life, a perseverance not often taught in city schools or families.

Xerxes' family was no stranger to the bad years. Nine years ago, Xerxes father was badly injured when the tractor slipped and rolled onto his left leg, leaving it crippled. Eight years ago, a new born child passed in its crib, only a few weeks old. Seven years ago, Xerxes became the 6th and last child for the Woodsons, Xerxes mother having died only a few days after his birth.

Xerxes oldest sibling, his only sister Naomi, tried her best to fill her mother's shoes for her younger brothers. Through chicken pox and the measles and colds and flus and scrapes and breaks she took care of them all, the best her young years allowed. But as happens to every young woman, a young man won her heart and carried her away. Xerxes felt the pang of this loss more acutely than his brothers because of his tender years and just when a mother's influence was most important in his life.

Now left on his own devices, a young man of Xerxes years would not have an appreciation for say, clean clothes or balanced meals, tidy surroundings or clean hands and face. And farm life being what it was, Xerxes father and older brothers were busy with working and schooling and their own lives and desires and maybe didn't pay enough attention to Xerxes.

So as the months after Naomi's wedding went past, Xerxes reverted into being a total boy, unclean, unkempt and uncaring. One night, while sleeping haphazardly on his unkempt bed in his little room downstairs, he was woken by a sharp pain on his wrist. When he got up and turned on the light, he discovered to his horror that his hands were covered in blood. Through a jolt of fear and incomprehension he ran upstairs to where his father lay snoring.

"Dad, Dad, you awake?" Xerxes ponderously asked from the doorway, the light from the hall's single hanging bulb outlining him. Parents of any ilk seem to have some supernatural sense when they are needed by one of their children and Xerxes father was immediately awoken.

"What's wrong, Xerx?" he asked tiredly. It had been common place for Xerxes to wake his father up at night in the first few weeks after Naomi's departure because of a nightmare or a night-time accident.

"Dad, my hands are covered in blood," Xerxes said on the verge of fearful tears, holding his arms out. I'm sure his father assumed this too was another nightmare, but as he sat up and reached for the light switch cord that dangled above the bed, he was shocked by what he saw. Xerxes hands were covered in blood. He jumped up out of bed and in two lopsided steps was kneeling at Xerxes side, holding his arms out to examine his son's hands. Unknowing disbelief clouded his sleep-fogged reasoning.

He turned Xerxes around. "Are you hurt anywhere else?" His father urgently asked, scaring Xerxes just a little more.

"N-n-no." Xerxes said barely controlling the tears now, as his father picked him up and limping, carried him across the hall and into the upstairs bathroom. When Xerxes' father examined his small son in the bright fluorescent light of the bathroom he noticed two small puncture wounds on the side of Xerxes' right wrist, set close together. He also finally noticed another thing; his son was filthy. Xerxes' hands encrusted with dried food and his face smudged with God knows what. It didn't take long to put all this together. A mouse, most likely drawn to Xerxes unkempt state bit Xerxes thinking he had found a new food source. Farms and mice go together like bread and butter. After he washed Xerxes' hands and arms and saw to stopping the tiny trickle of blood that was still oozing from the bite marks, he ran a bath for Xerxes. He commenced on extolling the virtues of cleanliness, feeling just a pang of guilt for his obvious ignorance of his youngest son's state of well-being.

Once Xerxes was cleaned and bandaged (farmers know how to take care of themselves) he walked Xerxes back down to his room. Upon seeing the sty that was passing as a bedroom he immediately sent Xerxes to wake up his two oldest brothers, Balthazar and Esau (their mother had had a penchant for unusual bible names). When they saw Xerxes had been hurt they also felt a twinge of guilt over their lack of attention to their youngest brother and they set to cleaning up without a grumble.

Conditions for Xerxes were nicely improved. His brothers made sure he had clean clothes, bathed regularly and that he kept his room neat. His father made sure he ate a sensible diet, heavy on carbs and fats like all farmers, with plenty of fresh vegetables. He got to school on time and had help with his homework. You might say, exterior conditions for Xerxes were vastly improved, almost back to pre-Naomi leaving times. But his interior condition was worsening daily.

He made sure he slept every night with his arms securely tucked under the covers, never dangling any part of his body off the bed at night. He used a flashlight to check the darker corners of his room for micely interlopers, those would-be assassins. He started to see mice where there wouldn't be mice, in the sock drawer (pair of rolled up grey socks) for example, or in the refrigerator and when he convinced Balthazar to extricate it, it turned out to be only a moldy avocado.

You could say mice, or at least the fear of mice, were taking over Xerxes life.

Now about this time his brother Boaz's class was reading a particularly well-known story about a fisherman and a whale. Boaz, a more bookish type than the rest of the brood, enjoyed talking about books and too much eye-rolling, launched into an explanation of the true meaning behind the story one night at the dinner table. Xerxes was all ears, but again being only seven may have missed the true gist of the story. That night in bed Xerxes spent long hours planning the extermination of his mousey nemesi.

His pogrom of mice extermination started the next day once he gathered up all the old mouse traps he had seen laying around in the sheds, barn and basement. With peanut butter jar in hand, he proceeded to lay as many traps around the house paying special attention to his own room for this perceived scourge, as he had working mechanisms. Mouse traps could now be found under the sofa and all the beds. Additional traps were laid in the darkest corners and behind large furniture. Several were strategically placed in the kitchen cabinets. In Xerxes mind, those little devils were goners.

Rising early the next morning Xerxes scurried around the house checking his traps for dead mice. To his disappointment though, all he found were a few snapped traps and one or two more with the alluring peanut butter eaten away. One lone mouse is all he caught, and that poor thing was still twitching. Xerxes, not knowing how to kill it, sadly left it to worry itself to death.

That night with his father off in town at a grange meeting with Balthazar and Esau, and his other brothers ensconced in their rooms, music or video games playing, Xerxes decided he had better redouble his efforts. He ran around the house resetting and re-baiting his traps with cheese and peanut butter, all the while liberally spilling large amounts of it on himself, in his haste. But he needed more traps. More traps equaled more dead mice, in Xerxes mind.

He scoured through the house for unused traps but found none. He braved the basement once again looking though all the dusty boxes and shelves for more traps, coming up only with two broken ones. Still carrying his cheese wedge and peanut butter jar he ran out to the barn, sure there would be more traps lurking in corners.

Now as I said before, farms and mice go together, especially in the barn. Mice love barns. In fact, Xerxes' father's barn had hundreds of mice living in its holes and shadows. Hundreds of hungry mice, anyone of which would love some peanut butter and cheese.

That night, as Xerxes was hunting mouse traps, he tripped and fell into the wall of the barn at the corner, smashing the peanut butter jar and spilling the cheese onto the floor. When Xerxes dizzily woke from the knock on his head it was already too late. Dozens and dozens of ravenous mice were almost upon him.

The End.

YORICK

If you've ever driven the back roads of the White or Green mountains in late winter/early spring you are sure to have noticed a peculiar thing in the woods. Seeming miles and miles of white tubing stretching up and up through the endless maple forests. For the first-time observer this is indeed a strange sight to behold, up and up and deep into the forest the tubing stretches connecting from tree to tree. From the days of the original natives, people have been collecting maple sap to produce a sweet flavorful syrup. Three types of maple trees can be tapped for sap, the Black and Sugar maples yield the sweetest sap, while the Red maple provides a less sweet sap.

One large maple tree can produce up to 20 gallons of sap, which after processing results in only two quarts of syrup. How is the sap from the Maple tree processed into syrup, you may wonder? In the easiest, if time consuming way – it is boiled down. The longer the water is boiled out, the sweeter the syrup becomes. Generally, it is boiled down until the sugar content is consistent at 67%, making for the sweet mapely treat you liberally drown your pancakes and waffles in.

One late autumn about twelve years ago, a young up and coming attorney in Tucson by the name of Frederick Neissen had taken on a client few others would have consented to as it was considered a losing case by almost everyone involved. The case involved murder, extortion and bribery committed (allegedly) by Mr. Neissen's new client. Through the use of supreme logic, deft investigation and a charming personality, Mr. Neissen was able to prove his client was innocent, in a very *Perry Mason* kind of way. Mr. Neissen had no use for legal flumoxxery or technicalities, if he proved you were innocent it was because you were innocent not because the cops or the prosecution skirted the law, mishandled evidence or otherwise didn't word their petitions correctly. Mr. Neissen dealt in absolutes. His clients were either innocent or guilty. If they were innocent, he got them off. If they were guilty, well he did their best for them, but they were still guilty.

Now Mr. Neissen came to the attention of a high-powered law firm in Bennington Vermont, who was on the lookout for an attorney of spotless character and record, to lead the defense of their innocent clients. They did just well defending their not so innocent clients themselves, in a *Boston Legal* kind of way. Because of a reputation of playing loosely with the spirit of the law, even when they defended an innocent client no one ever really believed it.

That is how Freddy (no one ever called him that more than once) and his wife, Judy found themselves driving through the Green Mountains of Vermont, looking for the new home they had rented online, which they liked so much they ended up buying and a few years later had their first child in, Yorick.

Lawyering can be a stressful profession. It is recommended that one take up an interesting and enjoyable hobby in one's spare time. Our friend Frederick took up golf, but in Vermont even the most ardent golfer can only play for about six months out of twelve so what to do with the winter months? Obviously, as the saying goes, make hay while the sun shines. Or in New England terms, make syrup while the sap runs. Frederick decided he wanted to make his own maple syrup.

It's easy enough. Step one – poke hole in tree. Step two - collect sap. Step three - boil sap until it tastes like maple syrup. Ta dah. And like the home brewer, and the bathtub gin maker, serious maple syrup producers are a breed of their own, don't ya know, ayup.

The seasons passed and Frederick developed a nice little cottage industry of making maple syrup. As Yorick got older Frederick shared this passion for syrup making with him. The selection of the trees to be tapped that season, the correct insertion of the spiel, the running of the sap lines from tree to tree and to the downhill collection area and most importantly, the art of boiling down the sap to just the correct temperature and consistency for syrup – these were the steps.

The large back yard of the house next to the small barn was dedicated in winter months to sap boiling. There were a dozen small boiling stations set up because Frederick believed small batches were best.

After the sap collection began, he and Yorick would clear out the fire pits, set up the supports that held the large, deep pans which the sap would be boiled in and would spend weekends making maple syrup. As the sap boiled down in each pan, more sap would be added until each pot contained about five gallons of syrup. Once cooled slightly, the pots would be carted into the barn and the newly boiled sap would be poured into smaller pans on the gas stovetop where Judy would watch the final boiling stage closely.

Once the new syrup passed Frederick's taste and consistency tests, all of it was filtered into large wooden barrels for storage until it was time for bottling.

One year when Yorick was about ten years old, a big murder case consumed Frederick's time all winter, even on the weekends. It being well past time for the tapping to have begun, Yorick finally convinced his father to let him go up into the hills and start tapping the trees. Because Frederick sorely missed his maple syrup making time and knew Yorick was anxious to prove himself, he consented.

As Yorick was in the barn one day in the early morning readying to commence, Frederick asked him, "What trees will you tap?"

"Only the sugar maples up on the far hill." Yorick dutifully answered, for they had been over this several times already.

"Remember, you can get the pits ready but don't start the boil until I say. The sap will keep fine in the outdoor collection tanks as long as the temperature stays below 38." It wasn't that Frederick didn't trust Yorick, it was that he was sorely missing the opportunity to engage in his favorite hobby along with him that made him seem so naggy.

"Yes, dad," Yorick patiently said with a hug for his father as he trudged out the door and through the snow, his pack of spiels and coils of tubing swinging along behind him.

Yorick spent that whole day up on the far hill identifying the best of the sugar maples and placing his spiels, all dutifully plugged until he connected the tubing to the downhill storage tanks. That first day Yorick tapped and connected almost a dozen trees before he returned home to warm up and eat. There was just one or two more Yorick wanted to tap tomorrow, then he could finish connecting the tubing and start the sap running.

Yorick was asleep in bed long before his father returned home that night after a long day in court. He was gratified to hear from his wife Judy how well Yorick seemed to have gotten along on his own today. He was looking forward to examining the tap line once completed. He went to bed a happy man, looking forward to his return to making maple syrup with his son Yorick as soon as this case finished.

The next day, Frederick was up and gone before Yorick rose. Over breakfast Yorick regaled his mother with stories of how he selected his trees yesterday, how deep the snow was this year up on the far hill and how he planned on tapping the two trees he identified yesterday.

After donning the appropriate winter gear, packing his bag with the needed spiels and tubing, Yorick set out from the barn toward the far hill like he did yesterday, with his mother waving from the kitchen window.

Yorick trudged through the hip deep snow along the same path he made yesterday, stopping to examine yesterday's work at all the trees he tapped and making sure everything with the tubing was tight. He continued on past his work area from yesterday and stepped up to a sugar maple he picked out for today, farther up the far hill.

As taught, Yorick used a specialty hammer to tap on the tree to listen for hollow spots or defects before he chose the spot to place the spiel. Yorick's father used particularly long spiels for his taps because he believed the deeper the better for the tapping of sap, so one had to be extra careful.

Yorick held the spiel into the chosen spot and commenced tapping on it with his hammer, like he had done so many times before. As Yorick pounded the spiel harder and harder into the hard wood of the maple tree deeper and deeper an unknown and unseen fault in the tree's interior caused a major weakness to give way to the weight of the tree above it, causing the whole tree to break in half and come toppling down. It had all happened so fast poor Yorick had no chance to jump clear through the heavy snow.

The End.

ZILLAH

Zillah lived with her ancient grandmother in a rundown and ramshackled house on the outskirts of a small town in eastern Czechoslovakia, when it was still one country. Back in the good old days, as Zillah's grandmother likes to remind people, she had been a burlesque dancer, young and beautiful and fleet of foot and form. She had married a wealthy merchant who had built a beautiful house for her. Unfortunately, this particular merchant had an eye for other beautiful young women also, and though Zillah's grandmother had a house maid and was rich by the town's standards, she was not very happy through the long years of her marriage.

One day very late in life, but many years before Zillah, Zillah's grandmother finally became pregnant with a child, and in due course gave birth to a beautiful baby boy. Even though the merchant's finances and business deals had faltered, these were the happiest days of her life. The young handsome boy was a joy to know and was doted on by the whole town. When the young man turned seventeen, he in turn took a young wife, and they set to producing their own child. This would become Zillah.

Now just about this time the young newly married man who would be Zillah's father was called away to fight in some border skirmish that had been ongoing for hundreds of years. Sadly, before he could learn that he was to become a father, he was killed on the battlefield. Upon hearing this terrible news, his young wife became so despondent she forgot the will to live and perished in child birth.

Zillah was born an orphan and would be raised solely by her once again unhappy grandmother, her grandfather having also disappeared. Many in the town say he just got up one day and walked away, but Zillah's grandmother wouldn't talk about it at all, so no one really knows.

As time passed and Zillah's little family become poorer and poorer, her grandmother grew unhappier and unhappier, finally giving in to the urge to stay drunk the whole day. Zillah's grandmother would sit morosely in the dark and dusty parlor, on the flower-patterned camel-back sofa purchased in Paris, drinking daily, mostly vodka, but anything would do in a pinch. To raise money for her habit, she started to sell off her and Zillah's only possessions, the home's antique furnishings.

At first, these items brought in quite a bit of coin, hers being the nicest house in town and the furnishings and what-nots coming from all over Europe. There were carpets and rugs from Iran and India, tables and chairs, sofas and stands, Tiffany bowls and Steuben vases and statues galore to sell. Eventually as the townsfolk bought all they needed, wanted or could afford, it became harder and harder to sell off the old stuff. There came a day when the cupboards were bare, the best of the furnishings mostly gone, and no hope in sight.

The neighbors knowing their plight did what they could to help out. Freshly picked vegetables would show up on the back stoop without warning, neighbors scurrying away, crossing themselves less some of the family's bad luck attract to them. Eggs and meats and cheeses would also appear randomly, wrapped in cloths or left in baskets, all with a little muttered prayer for protection from evil. Though this largesse was needed, it caused more and more despondency in Zillah's grandmother, who once was a beauty and one of the wealthiest people in town and now was looked upon as someone cursed and in need of charity so much misfortune had befallen her.

Zillah would amble off to school most days in her out of date hand me downs. Her shoes were usually too small and often mismatched, her long hair un-brushed and she would sit quietly in the back until it was time to hurry back home to the old, dark and dusty mansion and to her usually inebriated grandmother.

Zillah had few friends, well truth be told, she had none. The other children warned by their parents to avoid Zillah and the cursed grandmother, did just that. Zillah would go to school, sit by herself and then return home immediately to be alone. Sometimes her grandmother was still in that sweet spot between a buzz and totally drunk that she would call Zillah into the parlor and tell her stories of the better days. Zillah loved those days best, the days she could sit with her gram and hear about her father's childhood or her grandmother's dancing.

On the days she was left to her own devices she would go upstairs and fabricate complex fantasies in her mind with the help of her only doll, whom she named Zoe. She was a famous dancer, like her grandmother and Zoe was the adoring audience. She was a queen in a castle and Zoe was her worshipping subject. She was the mother, and Zoe her beautiful daughter whom she cared carefully for. She had tea parties at her little table, though there was no tea set or tea, Zoe the only guest. She would pretend they all lived as a happy family, grandmother, mother and father with Zillah and Zoe.

On the worst days, she would pretend she wasn't hungry and lonely.

One day a traveler came through town and headed straight to Zillah's house. He was an antiques dealer and found her grandmother in an alert state, it still being morning. Zillah was enraptured by this stranger who had invaded their lives, though she stayed mostly hidden behind her grandmother. After much looking around and poking through things he and her grandmother came to an understanding and much money was exchanged for many of the homes remaining treasures.

It was a happy day in Zillah's life that day as they immediately set off to the shops in the town center to purchase many things. Zillah got a new pair of shoes and a new hat, plus a pretty flowered dress she saw in the window. They bought pastries and candies, the like of which Zillah had never seen. They went to the green grocer and the butchers and stocked their pantry full, and they also went to the tavern and bought many bottles of vodka and whiskey and gin.

The news spread through the little town like a wildfire. Zillah and her grandmother were on a spending spree, buying out half the shops, so it seemed. The women of the town gathered and behind their hands clucked over every purchase, especially the liquor with a tsk, tsk, tsk.

There were happy days ahead for Zillah and her grandmother, with a kitchen stocked full, and a new dress to wear. Zillah's grandmother even walked Zillah to school the first few days after the largesse had fallen on them. But as time does, it wears things down and away and eventually her grandmother fell back into her daily alcohol fueled stupor, largely ignoring Zillah on most days.

One day after school, Zillah was having one of her famous tea parties with Zoe, regaling her yet again with a story about the day she and her grandmother went shopping, when she realized she could now provide herself and Zoe with a better tea party repast than normal.

Zillah scampered down the stairs, first to cast an eye on her grandmother, who by this time in the afternoon was quietly snoring on the divan in the parlor, then into the pantry to see what was still available. It had been sometime since the shopping day and the pantry was again starting to show signs of despair.

Zillah spied a tin of tea up on the high shelf but tea was difficult to make without being able to use the stove and Zillah was expressly forbidden from doing that. Down lower was a collection of half full liquor bottles just waiting to be used for a great tea party. She chose carefully from the selection offered, passing by something called 'becherovka' and ended up with something called 'gin'.

In her hurry to get upstairs to show her acquisition to Zoe, Zillah forgot to carry any actual cups or glasses up with her. 'No mind', she thought, 'I can just sip a little from the bottle.' Zoe was still sitting in her carefully arranged place at the table and Zillah set the bottle down between them. At this tea party, Zillah decided, she would be the town's wealthy lady and Zoe an adoring neighbor come to visit.

Zillah found the first few sips from the bottle to be a burning, terrible tasting thing but with Zoe's encouragement, she preserved until more than half the bottle was emptied.

That was Zillah and Zoe's last tea party.

The End.

About the Author

Matthew Woodruff is an award-winning magazine features writer and editor. Now on staff at the University of Florida he began working on this, his first book, in 2017. Shortly after the release of *'26 Absurdities'* he was awarded 'Author of the Month' by Self-Publisher's Showcase in September 2018. He enjoys creating works in the dark humor/dark fiction genre. He would like you to connect with him on social media and welcomes any comments or questions.

Friend me on Facebook: http://facebook.com/No1Books
Follow me on Twitter: http://twitter.com/WriterMatthewW
Connect on LinkedIn: http://www.linkedin.com/in/matthewcwoodruff
Visit my website: www.MattWoodruffAuthor.com

Libraries@Trocaire

CPSIA information can be obtained
at www.ICGtesting.com
Printed in the USA
LVHW101216231119
638278LV00007B/208/P

9 781720 861751